SWIMMING with DOLPHINS

SWIMMING with DOLPHINS

JESSIE PADDOCK

Scholastic Inc.

ISBN 978-1-338-53812-0

10 9 8 7 6 5 4 3 2 20 21 22 23 24

Printed in the U.S.A. 40

First printing 2020

Book design by Keirsten Geise

For all kids navigating unexplored oceans

Chapter 1

For probably the first time ever, we're silent. Cady, Kaytee, and I sit at our usual yellow table at Jake's Freeze, our favorite ice cream shop. In front of Cady sits a dish of soft-serve swirl with hot fudge. It looks like a melting volcano. Kaytee stabs a spoon into her cup of strawberry ice cream. I resist the urge to pick up a crayon and doodle on the scrap paper scattered among our scoops, because our attention is focused on something else: the empty chair parked at the end of the table.

At least a minute goes by. I fiddle with my left earring, a small silver stud in the shape of a dolphin. I got it for my birthday almost a year ago. I never take it off.

"This is hard." I sigh.

"Harder than the last chair-naming ceremony, for sure," Kaytee agrees. "But we got this."

"What about Beatrice?" Cady suggests.

"That makes her sound old," I say.

"More like *vintage*, but fine." Cady rolls her eyes, pretending to be annoyed. Cady and I often disagree, but we only love each other more for it.

I grin and take another lick of my cone: rocky road with chocolate sprinkles. Always rocky road with chocolate sprinkles. Jake's makes the best rocky road in all of Iowa City, and it's not just because his is the only ice cream shop with actual homemade ice cream. It sounds cheesy, but ice cream made with love . . . well, you get it.

"Sapphire?" Cady suggests.

"That wouldn't make sense. She's black and purple, not green," I say.

"Sapphires are blue," Kaytee reminds her gently.

"You both are so literal," Cady says.

"We're literal Libras," I joke.

We all chuckle. None of us knows much about astrology; just that our October birthdays make us all Libras.

"If we want to be accurate here, we need something that really implies 'girl-boss,'" Kaytee murmurs.

"Def," Cady and I agree in unison.

Again, we fall into silence. The one-day-out-of-the-box, good-as-new wheelchair practically sparkles in the early-afternoon light.

More silence.

Cady, Kaytee, and I have been BFFs for six years. C2K

Squad, we call ourselves, because Cady's name starts with a C, and Kaytee's and mine start with Ks. In addition to having the same name (despite different spellings), we all have October birthdays. We always have a joint birthday party. Not to brag, but our parties are the best. The. Best. Everyone knows it. Every year we pick a different theme, but the thing that makes them so fun is that everybody is invited. None of that nonsense where the "cool" kids exclude the "less cool" kids. The first year of our joint party we decided it was too stressful to even think about guest list politics. Come one, come all, and pretty much everyone comes. Afterward, the three of us always sleep over at my house, where my parents have a Rice Krispies Treat cake waiting.

We've been planning our upcoming thirteenth birthdays all summer long. It was going to be the most epic yet.

That was, until . . .

I try not to think about it. I grab a crayon. *Bluetiful,* the wrapper reads. I begin to sketch the only thing I ever really sketch. Mr. Jake equips every table in his shop with a jar of crayons and scrap paper. "Sketches and scoops go together like whipped cream and sundaes," he explained when I asked him about it years ago.

"She's really a beauty," I say, licking the few remaining sprinkles off the surface of my scoop.

"Hmm," Cady and Kaytee hum in agreement.

Out of the corner of my eye, I notice Mr. Jake wiping off a nearby table. After Cady and Kaytee, I think I will miss Mr. Jake the most. I've spent countless hours at Jake's Freeze. On Friday nights, it is *the* place to be. My ice cream order hasn't changed in years, but he always lets me come behind the counter to look at any new special flavors anyway. The ledge on the customer-facing side of the freezer is just a few inches too tall for me to see over, but around back, where the scoopers stand, the edge doesn't come up as high and I can peer inside, no problem. I've been a certified VIP at Jake's since I won the Name the Flavor contest when I was in second grade. Dolphin Leap, a delicious mix of blueberry and vanilla cream, stayed on the menu that whole year. I always thought I'd get a job scooping ice cream for Mr. Jake the summer I turned fourteen.

I push the thought out of my head.

This concentrated silence is starting to get to me. "We can talk about something else," I say. "I don't want to take up our final minutes together stressing about a name. We should be thinking about our outfits for the first day of school." *Not that they're going to see mine,* I think. I won't be going into seventh grade with Kaytee and Cady. Iowa City Middle for them, and Fernbank Middle School, all the way down in Florida, for me. That's right: No hope of being in the same English class, no chance at arriving at our first seventh-grade dance arm in arm, definitely not going to Resurrect Summer . . . this list goes on.

"Don't be silly!" Kaytee interjects. "This is important."

"Yeah, team effort," Cady confirms.

My heart smiles. I love my friends.

"It's got to be the perfect name." Cady furrows her brow; that's her thinking face. "Show some Midwestern flair to those kids down in Florida."

It took less convincing than I expected for my parents to get me this chair. Not like they would deny me a wheelchair. It's how I get around, after all. Always have, always will. But this one is super fancy. Like, less than twenty pounds, state-of-the-art, and even comes in my favorite color. Major upgrade. A brand-new chair would have been out of the question (wheelchairs aren't cheap). But Mom is a pro at finding great deals online.

My old chair, Wiggles, wasn't necessarily ready to officially retire, though she was looking a little battered around the edges. I didn't put it quite this way—I have manners, of course—but since Mom and Dad are moving us all the way to Fernbank, Florida, less than sixty days before my thirteenth birthday, with basically no warning, away from everything I know and love, I figured a spiffy new ride wasn't too much to ask for. I was born and raised in Iowa City, so I don't know a ton about being the new kid, but I'm pretty sure that showing up on the first day of seventh grade in a clunky, not-so-polished chair would be a major faux pas.

"I got it," Cady begins. I tear my eyes from my drawing—not my best work, but not my worst, either—and focus on Cady. She looks determined. "Priscilla!"

"That sounds like a doily," I say with a giggle. Kaytee shakes her head and laughs.

"Or a princess," Cady insists. "But now that I think about it, my cousin Priscilla acts like a total princess, and not in the cute or vintage way, so scratch that."

"This beautiful hunk of rubber and steel and glory deserves a name as beautiful and glorious and strong as KT herself," Kaytee says.

"Yes, and as *Libra-y* as KT herself," Cady agrees.

"And as rubbery and steely. I'm as rubbery and steely as they come." I flex my arm muscles and growl. We all start giggling, and then full-on laughing because without even saying anything we know that I'm referencing the time Enrique gave me a Valentine that was actually a stick figure drawing of him flexing.

The cell phone in my lap buzzes. A text from Lucy, my big sister, pops up: 5 away.

"I'm really going," I say. I was hoping this was all a dream that would just evaporate before it was too late.

As if they're reading my mind—because, let's be honest, both Kaytee and Cady can basically read my mind—Cady throws her arm over my shoulder and Kaytee reaches across the table and takes hold of my free hand.

"Nothing is going to change," Kaytee assures me. "Well, okay, like literally everything is going to change, but that's only on the outside. On the inside, we're the same. C2K Squad for life."

I nod, but I feel tears rushing from that place where they hide, deep behind my eyeballs. I blink them away quickly and pop the final bite of my cone into my mouth.

"Sorry, I don't mean to be dramatic," I say, once I finish chewing.

Cady nearly cuts me off. "I don't think shedding a tear at a time like this counts as dramatic."

"Yeah," Kaytee says softly. "You can cry. We promise we won't watch."

That makes me smile.

"I feel like I'm moving to a postcard. Is it even real down there?" I've only ever seen pictures of the ocean, never seen it in real life. "All those photos look fake. The palm trees and Kool Aid–colored water and sea animals jumping all over the place can't actually exist, right?"

"Don't act like you don't want to see dolphins leaping out of that water. That's, like, your dream," Cady says.

"You're not wrong," I admit.

"There we go. Three points for Florida," Kaytee says, always the optimist. "Good one, by the way." Kaytee points to the *blueti-ful* dolphin I've absentmindedly drawn. The dorsal fin is a little off, if you ask me, but it's definitely still a dolphin. It's fitting that I am a genius at drawing my favorite animal.

"Look," Cady begins, "sorry-not-sorry to brag, but I'm only like ten thousand subscribers away from becoming YouTube famous."

Kaytee and I roll our eyes. Cady has been pushing hard for YouTube fame all summer. In June she was all about makeup tutorials, but then her mom caught her and said twelve is way too young to wear eyeliner. I helped her film a gazillion videos of her performing Shakespeare-inspired sonnets I had written from the perspective of her dog. This past month she decided to invent her own victory dance that will be so hilarious all college players will want to use it when they score, and then they'll have to pay her a fee or something. I don't totally follow the logic, but she's convinced. I wish I were going to be here next month to see what ridiculous slash completely hilarious idea she comes up with next.

"Seriously!" Cady shouts. "The second I get my first sponsor, I'm buying Kaytee and me first-class tickets to come see you. We'll all be teenagers by then and it will be great."

I inhale, and a loose sprinkle falls onto the table. I resist the urge to eat it. I need to spit out what I've been thinking about since the moment I knew I was leaving. I can't avoid it any longer.

"You should still have the party."

"Are you crazy?!" Kaytee says, almost spitting out a mouthful of strawberry ice cream.

Cady drops her spoon into a hunk of hot fudge, leans back, crosses her arms, and gives me her tough look. Kaytee is near tears and Cady appears ready to rumble. Typical. I can't help but crack a smile. I love how well I know my best friends.

"I'm serious," I insist. "Just because I won't be there doesn't mean you both won't be turning thirteen. Not celebrating a birthday is like a cardinal sin. Plus, Resurrect Summer is way too good of a theme to bail on."

The irony that I'm moving to a place where it's practically always summer is not lost on me.

"That is so not the point," Cady challenges.

"We could never do it without you," Kaytee continues, which is exactly what I need to hear.

"Besides, what would be the fun of throwing a big birthday party if you didn't argue with me about the decorations?" Cady adds.

"I still can't believe you wanted us to make forty mermaid tails by hand that time," I say with a laugh.

"Nothing beats homemade decor!" Cady claims.

We dissolve into giggles. The kind of laughter that makes your stomach hurt, but also isn't all that different from crying, either.

The cowbell over the door clanks behind me. Lucy's arrived. I know it's her by the look on Cady's and Kaytee's faces. Even after six solid years of BFFship, they still blush when Lucy is within earshot. No matter how many times I tell them that Lucy is quiet because she's shy—not because she's mean; she is basically the biggest softie ever, who would rather play video games than be mean to twelve-year-olds—they can't get over being intimidated by my big sister.

I feel a tug on the back of my strawberry-blond fishtail braid.

"Hey, KT Lady," she says. "Hey, other Katies."

"Hi!" my friends chirp in unison.

"I hate to break up the party. Oh, and, K, you have sprinkles on your lip," she says. I wipe what feels like more sprinkles than is humanly possible off my mouth with the back of my hand. I'm not embarrassed. All present company know I'm a messy sprinkle eater and that's all there is to it. That's when it hits me.

"OMG–Sprinkle! That's it!" I exclaim.

"Sprinkle!" Kaytee and Cady repeat.

"You love sprinkles! It's perfect!" Kaytee confirms.

"It's not too . . ." My voice trails off as I search for the right word. "I don't know . . . flashy for her?" I say, waving my fingers in the air. What I really mean is, is it too flashy for *me*?

"No way. It's perfect," Cady says.

"Perfect. For both you *and* your new chair," Kaytee adds.

Cady claps. "More perfect than perfect!"

I'll take their word for it.

"Sprinkle it is!" I say, relieved to finally make a decision. It's not right to use a chair before giving her a proper name. Everybody knows that.

"Okay, you goofballs, I don't exactly know what you're talking about, but, KT, Mom and Dad are trying to get on the road before the next touchdown. Dad thinks it's bad luck to begin a road trip while we're in the end zone, for some reason."

Lucy and I share a good-natured eye roll. My parents are obsessed with Iowa Hawkeyes sports, football in particular, as are most people in Iowa City. I'm surprised they even considered living somewhere outside the range of the local radio station. I don't totally care about football—I know for a fact those helmets don't protect players very well—but I do love that everybody in Iowa City has something big to care about together. Even if it is football.

I'm about to scootch from my seat at the end of the booth and onto Sprinkle when my dolphin doodle catches my eye. Along with coloring supplies on every table, Jake's has a bulletin board by the register where anyone can pin up their artwork. On

Sundays the wall resets, so it's like a rotating gallery. Though my drawing skills don't extend much beyond aquatic life (fish, seaweed, and shellfish are also among my specialties), I gotta represent the Wynn family. I always tack up my dolphin du jour on the right side closest to the window, but today—my last day at Jake's Freeze with my two best friends in the entire world—I have a better idea. I grab another crayon, something in the violet family. I scrawl out *C2K 4 LYFE* above the dolphin, then tear the drawing in half. One for Cady, one for Kaytee. I hand them over.

"For life," I whisper.

Maybe I'm being dramatic, but I'm not alone. As we hug goodbye, we hide our tears from no one.

After the waterworks die down, Lucy nudges me. It really is time to go. On my way out, I make sure to catch Mr. Jake's attention.

"How was your cone?" he asks.

"A-plus." I give him a high five. Mr. Jake is the oldest and kindest person I know. He's had his shop since my parents were students at the University of Iowa, aka a million years ago.

"You better send us some sunshine from Florida come December," he says.

I manage a smile even though something about his request makes my heart ache a bit more than it already does.

"Okay. Express mail," I promise.

Mr. Jake gives my head a pat and then leans down for a hug. He smells like sweet cream and peanut butter.

He says, "I'll miss you, Rocky Road with Chocolate Sprinkles."

I'll miss you, too, I want to say, but no words come out. I just hold on tight.

Chapter 2

The farthest I've been from Iowa City is Des Moines (I used to go there a lot for physical therapy), but to get to Florida, we have to drive in the opposite direction. I imagine I'm a bird flying above us, watching our white minivan, Beluga, speed down the interstate. Lucy and I named it Beluga for obvious reasons. From up in the sky, I wouldn't see the scratches on the side door and the dent on the bumper. To a bird, it would look like the Wynn family is traveling southeast inside a cloud.

My parents listen to the radio announcer describe the game like their lives depend on it. Lucy has her earbuds in, which means she's officially in zombie mode. She's been doing this thing lately where she puts her headphones on at totally inappropriate times, like at dinner or when I'm trying to get her opinion on a new outfit combination. Rude. I overheard Mom on the phone once saying, "That's just what teenagers do." I'm not sure if she was talking about the headphones or something else. When I'm a teenager in a few weeks, will I automatically be moody for no reason and act like I'm bored when in public? Hope not.

I have the opinion section of the newspaper on my lap, in addition to an article I printed out about a newly discovered species of river dolphin in South America. I'm not ready to read just yet, though. I lightly drum my fingers on my knee and stare out the window. Time to brace myself for the T minus 18 hours when corn and soybean fields become palm trees and whatever else grows on the Gulf Coast.

"Don't worry, KT Lady. There's no snow in Florida." That was the first thing Lucy said after Mom and Dad broke the news. She probably saw the look on my face. I'm an expert at not letting myself show emotions that I think will scare people or make them pity me or just seem annoying in general, but in that moment I couldn't hide my total and complete devastation. Lucy jumped in quickly. She knows how much I hate Iowa City winters. Snow plus ice plus a metal wheelchair that retains subzero temperatures like no other? No. Thank. You.

I thought Lucy would be really bummed to spend her senior year of high school somewhere different, but she was up for the change. Not like we had a choice. Mom had no chance of making tenure at the University of Iowa because of "department politics," as she put it (she's a psychology professor), and Dad was recently laid off from his main job at Pugh's Electrics when the company downsized. When Mom got a professor position at Fernbank College, she had no choice but to accept. Or at least that's how they put it. You always have a choice, though. Unless you got into an accident when you were a toddler that made you paralyzed from the waist down.

Ha. That was a joke.

I hope kids in my new school will think a joke like that is funny. Cady and Kaytee always got it.

I start seventh grade in less than a week. I've never been the new kid, but we've had plenty of new kids come through Iowa City. Lots of professors would come to town with their families when they were hired to teach at the university. I stare out the window, watching the cornfields whir by, trying to remember the kinds of questions we asked the newbies over the years. I prepare answers of my own.

Yes, I've lived in Iowa City my whole life. Sure, it gets cold in the winter, but that makes spring sweeter. And yes, there's a lot of corn. Soybeans, hay, and oats, too. But it's the best place in the world. Some streets have cobblestones, which make for a bouncy ride, but they're really pretty, or *vintage*, as Cady would say. People are friendly, except for Kevin Cholula and Isaiah Green. Everybody knows everybody, but that's not necessarily a bad thing. In fact, it's kind of nice.

Of course I miss my friends. Cady, Kaytee, and I have been

BFFs since first grade. I know it's crazy that we all have the same name. No, it's not annoying, and not the reason why I spell my name "KT" instead of "Katie."

I want to be a reporter when I grow up (is this something they'll even ask?). I like to be the first one to find out information, plus I'm very observant. I know how to pay attention to the world around me. An important quality in a reporter.

And then all the obvious and hopefully not too silly questions: Do I remember the accident? Does it hurt my butt to sit down all the time? Can I feel my feet? No, no, no, but that doesn't mean I can't wear cool shoes.

Mom always says, "Helping others feel heard is a key to interpersonal connection." In other words, I can't just answer questions. I'll have to ask some, too. I'm sure I'll have plenty. Starting with, "How does it feel to live in a postcard?"

What else?

I yawn. I know there's so much I haven't thought of yet, but the buzz of Beluga's engine lulls me to sleep.

* * *

After six hours on the road, we park at a motel for the night. Even though we had to stop several times for me to change positions and shift my weight in my chair (so I don't get bedsores), and another two for Lucy to pee (smallest bladder ever), Mom says we've made decent time. Lucy and I share one bed,

Mom and Dad the other. Everyone seems to fall asleep right away except for me. To help wind down, I make a list in my mind.

There are some pluses to this situation, sure:

- As Lucy said, it doesn't snow in Florida. That comes up a lot, but it's a big one.
- I'll finally get my own bedroom. Everyone wants their own bedroom, right?
- Mom's and Dad's work situations will be much better. Dad's already hooked up with an electrician gig, too. I know that will make them calmer.

Three great pluses, but that's not very many at all. Now for the minuses. There's, like, a ton of those:

- No Cady and no Kaytee.
- No Jake's Freeze or Mr. Jake.
- No Chloe, Romulo, Maddox, Jayden, David R., David M., Maria, Ruwa, or Marina. They are my second-tier friends. I don't mean that in a bad way. I've known most of them since I was in first grade. We would always say hi in the hallways or when we run into each other at the farmers' market.
- No Mrs. Reynolds, the librarian. I've always been

impressed by her consistency (she taught me that word when I came to check out books three days in a row). She rarely smiles unless you ask her about Louie, her pet dachshund. Also, I've caught her reading complicated-looking graphic novels behind her desk at least seven times. That's rad.

- No East Jefferson Street, where all the houses look haunted but in an exciting way.
- No Julie's Attic Thrifts, where there's extra-wide aisles (unlike the Goodwill) and old CDs for one dollar. Now that I think about it, Julie's is where Cady's obsession with all things vintage began.
- No hope of ever waking up to snow on Christmas morning.
- No more listening to Lucy snore from the top bunk. Lucy insists she doesn't snore, not even when she has allergies, but I know the truth. I've never minded her snoring, anyway. It reminds me that she's right there. Tonight, in this stuffy motel, is the last night we'll be sleeping in the same room. She's not snoring. Yet.

Even though I'm working on the minus list, another plus pops to mind. Sort of. I remember what Kaytee joked back at Jake's. I won't get to celebrate my thirteenth birthday with the two best friends that ever existed (minus), and my second-tier friends along with all the other familiar faces from Iowa City Middle School won't be there either (minus), and I can't resurrect summer because it will basically be summer in Florida constantly (minus for Florida, sort of plus for warm weather). But dolphins live in Florida. Maybe, after all these years of studying, daydreaming about, and drawing dolphins, I'll finally get to see one.

Maybe.

That would be cool. A plus, for sure.

But you don't need to move to Florida to see a dolphin. You just need to go on vacation.

Chapter 3

We arrive at our new home thirty-four hours after leaving Iowa City. The one-story house looks just like the pictures, actually. The outside is painted light brown, and the shutters are white. The front door is yellow. There's not one but *two* palm trees in the front yard, as if to prove that we really are in Florida. One is small and fat and the other is super, super tall and skinny, and bends at a concerning angle. The golden-hour light makes our new house look kind of peaceful.

Peaceful, but not home. Not yet.

While my parents unload Beluga, I roll to the end of the driveway to get a wide view of our new house, straining to find a detail that feels familiar.

"KT, don't go into the street," Mom says. I swear she has eyes in the back of her head. I'm a good four feet from the end of the driveway. "Lucy, why don't you go pick up some dinner for us?" Mom tosses Lucy the keys to Beluga. Lucy got her license three months ago and takes any opportunity she can to drive, even if it's running errands for Mom and Dad. "I saw a Chinese place on the main road just a couple minutes back. Should we get the usual?"

I wonder if lo mein, sesame chicken, and egg drop soup taste the same down here.

"Or we could get burgers from this place called Tommy's," Lucy says, reading from her phone. "'Home of Fernbank's Original Double-Double.'"

"Do they have milkshakes?" I ask.

"What kind of burger place doesn't have milkshakes?" Lucy asks sarcastically.

"Tommy's, Tommy's, Tommy's!" I chant. I love ice cream in any form.

"Where is it? I didn't notice it on our way," Mom says as she pulls two huge contractor bags from Beluga's trunk. They're overflowing with towels and sheets.

"Le Google Maps says it's just on the other side of the highway."

"Hmm."

"That's only fifteen minutes. Straight shot," Lucy argues.

"I don't know. You're not familiar with the roads here yet."

I've learned not to take it personally when Mom acts all overprotective of me, because she's like that with Lucy, too. She's like that with everybody, actually. Me, Lucy, Cady, Kaytee, probably her students. She's just a worrier. Years of educating, she says, which I guess makes sense.

"Ma, c'mon, it's really no big—"

"She'll be okay," Dad says, grabbing the last gigantic bin from the trunk.

A moving company will deliver our big stuff, like furniture, tomorrow morning, but we still stuffed Beluga to the brim with the essentials.

Mom exhales and gives in. "Fine. Text me when you get there."

"Okaaay," Lucy says, drawing out the last syllable. She mouths a thank-you to Dad, and he winks back at her. "KT Lady, Sprinkle, you're coming."

Dad pulls the last bags out of the car, and after I've scootched myself into the passenger seat, Lucy swiftly breaks down Sprinkle and loads her into the trunk. I buckle my seat belt and Lucy jumps behind the wheel. My stomach grumbles. I'm ready to inhale a chocolate milkshake, appetizer style.

* * *

Twenty minutes later, we still haven't found Tommy's. In fact, I don't see any places that look like they sell food.

"Are you sure you know where we're going?" I ask Lucy.

"Totes. Text Mom from my phone and say there's a long line, but it's worth it because the burgers smell sooo good."

I look at Lucy. She has what would definitely be described as a sneaky grin on her face.

"What are you up to? Are we driving back to Iowa?" I'm only half kidding.

"Just do what I say." She pauses, and then whispers, which seems over the top considering we're the only two people in the car. "Sister Secret. It'll be worth it."

That seals the deal. There's almost nothing I wouldn't do for a Sister Secret. I don't like to lie to Mom, but there's basically no traffic out here, and Lucy is a way-above-average teenage driver (according to her, at least). I type out the text.

In Iowa City, my favorite burger was from the Hamburg Inn. It was greasy and delicious. I'd always get it with sweet potato fries and baked beans. I bet Tommy's doesn't have baked beans.

I'm about to press send when a new text comes in from her BFF, Jade: Change can be good!

I like Jade, but I'm not sure she has any idea what she's talking about.

"Sent?" Lucy asks. I glance her way but don't say anything. "If you're chicken, I'll do it," she says, that fun-loving sneaky, sneaky, sneaky look on her face again, which is how I know we're about to do something kind of not allowed, but definitely worth it. She reaches to grab her phone out of my hand.

"Hey, no texting while driving!" I say, switching the phone to my right hand, out of her reach. I quickly send the text to Mom and drop the phone in the cup holder. "Done!"

"Good work," she says. "Now close your eyes." My heart dances and I obey. Lucy turns up the radio, and I feel the warm wind from the open window twirl against my face. "No peeking."

Five minutes later, Beluga is parked and my eyes are still closed, which makes getting from my seat to Sprinkle a little more complicated. The air feels heavy on my skin, but maybe that's just because we've stopped. I hear some birds squawking in the distance, and it seems very quiet, but also not. It's hard to explain.

"Keep them closed just a minute longer." Lucy takes Sprinkle and me over what is definitely asphalt, and then what could possibly be a gazillion bobby pins scattered over the ground. Then we kind of sink into something soft and stop.

I hear Lucy take a deep breath. "Welcome to our first official Sister Secret, Florida edition." I hear the smile in her voice. She exhales. "Surprise!"

I open my eyes and gasp.

People who have never been to Iowa before always say that the sky is big and wide and open. I've never heard anyone compare the Iowa horizon to the ocean, but it's obvious the two landscapes have a lot in common. Staring at the sea now feels familiar. Big. Open. Wide. Free.

Like home.

The sun is setting, filtering through some distant pancake clouds. They glow Crayola Goldenrod, Razzle Dazzle Rose, and Neon Carrot. The turquoise water twinkles and goes on forever. Flecks of fading light look like lily pads on the ocean surface. I've never seen anything like it.

We don't speak for a little while. Lucy stands beside me and runs her fingers through the ends of my tangled hair. The air is thick, but not still.

"It's going to be okay here," Lucy finally says, so quietly I almost don't hear her. "You're going to be great. *We're* going to be great. It's all going to be really, really great."

I can tell she believes it, so I try my best to believe it, too.

We stay looking at the ocean longer than it could possibly take to receive four fast-food burgers, even if they had to ship the meat from Iowa. We don't say much, but we don't have to.

Suddenly, Lucy exclaims, "Did you see that?!"

"What?" I've been in a daze. I never want to stop looking at the ocean. It's just as hypnotizing as watching a roaring fire.

"Dolphin, nine o'clock! Or a shark, maybe."

"They don't have sharks here, do—"

"Right there!"

I see it now. One fin and then two slice through the surface of the water. I immediately reach for Lucy's hand because that seems like the right thing to do when you're lucky enough to see your very first dolphins, and your very first ocean, with your big sister all in the same day.

"Wow. Florida is really . . ." Lucy doesn't finish her thought.

"Postcard-y."

"Super postcard-y."

And for the first time, that doesn't seem like such a bad thing.

Chapter 4

Even though Lucy's Sister Secret was pretty much the best thing ever, I haven't been able to stop thinking about the text I saw. *Change can be good.* It makes me sad, and I'm not totally sure why. What Kaytee would call *melancholy*, maybe. But then I start feeling guilty that I saw Jade's text. And then I get kind of angry that she's offering advice when for all I know she has no idea what it's like to move to a new state and leave your life behind. And then I feel sad slash melancholy, guilty, and angry all over again.

What's so good about change? That's basically the opposite of what I believe.

The first two days in Florida have been boring, boring, boring. Mom and Dad are obsessed with unpacking and setting up the Internet and making sure the electricity is on. They're such grown-ups. The house is all one floor, no carpet, and they had most of the doorways widened before we arrived, so there's not too much to adjust for Sprinkle and me. Our furniture was delivered yesterday. It looks strange in our new house, like it doesn't belong to us. I have no friends to hang out with, so I've been lurking around the house. Lucy's determined to get to some new level or beat a boss in this video game she downloaded, so she's been glued to her computer in video zombie mode (technical term). In a moment of pure desperation, I asked Lucy to show me the ropes of her game. Unlike Mom, Lucy isn't the greatest teacher. After a few minutes, I'm a little bored and very confused. I excuse myself and leave her to it.

The vibe in our new house feels full-on mopey. Despite her video game goals, I can sense Lucy is a little low herself. I wanted to take Sprinkle out for a spin, but Mom said I couldn't go farther than the corner. In Iowa City there was a market at the end of our street that sold candy and sodas, so a limitation like this wouldn't have been so bad. But the closest gas station to our new house is not within wheelable distance. It's way too hot outside to make it very far, anyway. So we return home, where, thankfully, the air-conditioning works like a charm.

The final week of summer is officially a bust.

* * *

The last Saturday morning before school starts, I'm watching a really old movie about teenage vampires on my computer when Mom and Dad call for Lucy and me to join them in the kitchen.

"We have a surprise for you girls," Mom says.

I hoist myself off my bed and onto Sparkle. It crosses my mind that they're taking us to the beach, which means I'll have to remember to *act* surprised when we get there. They have no idea that there was no line at Tommy's the other night (in fact, it was empty) and Lucy took me to see the ocean. I'm not going to be the one to give our secret away.

Sister Secrets are like promises; they can't be broken.

I catch my reflection in the mirror that's temporarily been propped against the wall opposite my bed, and I take a moment to practice different surprised-face reactions. I could be an actor, I think.

"What are you doing with your face?" I hear Lucy ask.

"Nothing!" I swivel to see her standing in the doorway to my bedroom. Her extra-big black sunglasses sit on top of her head, and she has her extra-big gold headphones around her neck. Extra confusion in her expression, if I'm being honest.

"Weirdo."

Sometimes Lucy gets in a mood if her video game isn't going well or if she's just being a mysterious teenager. I've learned not to take it personally. I've also learned how to break her out of it.

"The weirdest," I say, making a signature KT Wynn face, the one where I pretend to catch a bubble in my mouth and bat my eyelashes.

Lucy makes the same bubble-mouth face back, then laughs.

Maybe it's the sunglasses or maybe it's just Florida, but for a moment Lucy looks older than seventeen. Together, we go to our new kitchen.

"Think of these as little Welcome to Florida bonuses," Mom says as she pushes a thick white envelope across the kitchen table to me. Dad hands Lucy a box wrapped in the local newspaper, the *Star-Banner Tribune*. I haven't gotten myself to read any articles from it yet. I watch Lucy tear open her present.

"Volleyball gear, sweet!" she says, taking a fresh pair of sneakers and clunky kneepads out of a shoebox.

"Since when are you into volleyball?" I ask.

Lucy grins, pulling a kneepad over her foot. "Since now." Then she shrugs and adds, "Change is good." I wonder if Jade knows about Lucy's new athletic dreams.

The white envelope Mom gave me isn't sealed, so when I flip it over I can see a tri-fold brochure and a slip of white paper bursting out. I remove the paper first. It appears to be a receipt. I silently read the words to myself.

Order Confirmation.

1 x Shadow a Trainer for a Day

Thanks for booking with Dolphina Cove. Your order AT1224L03 is confirmed.

I scan the remainder of the page. Something about a waiver and sun protection; the print is small and dense. I feel a flip in my stomach that reminds me of the first time I remember seeing snow.

I glance across the table at my parents. They watch me with closemouthed grins, like they're waiting to burst. I return to the words on the page, and more snowy butterflies tingle my stomach.

"What in the world . . . ?" My voice trails off as I take the brochure from inside the envelope. A moment later it hits me, and my jaw actually drops.

"No way!" I shriek. I'm nearly hyperventilating now, but in a good way.

"Way," Mom confirms.

"Double way," Dad adds.

"Wheeee!" Lucy adds for good measure. I just now notice she's been reading over my shoulder.

"Me? Them? For real?" My mind moves too fast to make complete sentences. Mom is smiling big. So is Dad. I feel Lucy's soft breath on my cheek as she continues to peer at the brochure. "Like, those right there?" I motion to the glossy photograph of a perfect, joyful dolphin. Above the picture, *Dolphina Cove: Florida's Oldest Dolphin Sanctuary* is written in spunky turquoise lettering.

"Yep," Dad says. "A whole day with real, live—"

"Dolphins!" I actually throw my hands in the air, I'm so happy.

“Ouch,” Lucy says, standing up and covering her ear closest to me. “Indoor voice, please.”

“Sorry,” I quickly apologize. Now is not the time for one of her moods. Not when possibly the most amazing thing that has ever happened to me is about to happen.

“I’M GOING TO MEET A DOLPHIN!”

My parents laugh. “Probably more than one,” Mom confirms. “The Trainer for a Day program looks really thorough. You might get to meet them all!”

“I’m going to meet a pod!” I cheer. “A pod is like a family of dolphins, by the way.”

“Obvi,” Lucy acknowledges, pulling another kneepad over her socked foot.

I quickly examine the description beneath the *Trainer for a Day* heading. Holy moly.

Now I whisper, because some things are too important to yell. “I get to swim with them, too?”

“That’s part of it,” Dad says. He looks almost jealous.

“Thank you thank you thank you!” I shout. “This is the best possible Florida bonus slash early birthday present ever.”

Okay, I’m not going to lie. I knew that dolphin centers or whatever were a thing. But I wasn’t sure if they were actually legit. I don’t live under a rock; I’ve seen a documentary or two and know what went down at SeaWorld with the orcas. But Mom and Dad promised that Dolphina Cove is totally humane, and it's actually more of a rescue center slash sanctuary than a creepy water-animal entertainment park. The dolphins are kept in an open-water lagoon, not pools or tanks (phew), so it's just like an extension of their natural habitat.

After my heart rate has decelerated a bit, I check out Dolphina Cove's website on my phone.

The graphics are a little shaky. Definitely one of the more outdated websites I've ever seen. But once all the pictures load, I'm kind of hooked. In every single photo, the dolphin is smiling. I think of the dolphins Lucy and I saw at the beach. I get the feeling I know exactly what dolphin skin feels like when you touch it. I bet it's rubbery, but also kind of soft. I can't wait to see if I'm right. This Dolphina Cove thing may be super postcard-y, but it's also going to be fun.

I'm really ready for some fun.

Chapter 5

The next morning Mom and I arrive at Dolphina Cove. Gravel rumbles beneath Beluga's tires as we pull into the parking lot at eight thirty sharp.

Boy, does Dolphina Cove have one stunning parking lot. Okay, the gravel is pretty standard (and pretty annoying—I don't want to beat up Sprinkle's tires before the first day of school), but the lush surroundings make up for it. Bright orange and purple flowers burst from the vines that line the lot's perimeter. The main building is light pink—the shade of a Brazilian river dolphin, to be exact—with white trim, and looks as if it's right out of a Caribbean fairy tale.

I snap a few photos with my phone as Mom unloads my chair from the trunk. She's had more practice, but she's not as quick as Lucy at putting Sprinkle back together. I want to capture every moment of this experience. My birthday is in exactly forty-eight days. Pretty sure today could be the actual highlight of my pre-teenager life. I want to be certain there's proper documentation.

Mom pushes me up the ramp to the reception center, then holds the door as I wheel myself inside. A woman sits behind a tall white desk, but I can only see her from the eyes up. She has white-blond hair and a forehead that look like it's been in the sun too long. She wears a pink visor even though we're inside. We seem to be the only visitors.

"We're here for the Trainer for a Day program," Mom announces to the woman.

"You must be KT," she exclaims. Her Southern accent is thick. Those will take me a while to get used to; they're very different from the accent back in Iowa. She stands to introduce herself. "My name is Annie, and we're so happy to have you here at Dolphina Cove!"

She's very chirpy. But then again, she does get to hang out around dolphins for a living, so I can't blame her. I notice her nails are painted light purple. When she smiles, she smiles big. One of her front teeth is slightly gray.

Annie explains a bunch of stuff about sun protection, bathrooms, and a waiver, but I'm hardly listening. I gaze at photographs around the office of happy Dolphina Cove visitors in the water, high-fiving dolphin fins, kissing them on the nose (sanitary?), and generally smiling their butts off. Seriously, I've never seen humans look so happy as they do in these pictures. Maybe I'll get my photo on the wall, too.

"Do I get to do that?" I ask, pointing to a particularly dramatic image of a little kid being pulled through the water by a dolphin's dorsal fin.

"You are going to have the *best* day."

I smile, but it's not lost on me that she didn't exactly answer my question. I also notice that she's looking at Mom as she talks to me. It's not the first time this has happened.

"Are you excited?" Annie asks in a high pitch.

"Extremely," I say, making my voice a little lower than usual. I do this sometimes when grown-ups talk to me like I'm a baby. It happens all the time, actually. Mom squeezes my shoulder and I shoot her a smile. *It's okay*, my smile says.

"Fantastic. Let's go out back." Annie gestures to the exit behind me.

I turn and head toward the glass door that obviously leads to a big deck.

"Oooh wee! You better slow down or you're going to get a speeding ticket!" Annie bellows jokingly.

"Vroom, vroom," I reply without looking back. I hear Annie catch her breath before she laughs. When we get to the exit I smack the silver button that opens the doors automatically. While we wait I look up at Annie and smile. As I expected, that seems to put her a bit more at ease, which makes everything easier. Nervous grown-ups are just a handful.

“You’ve got some spunk!” Annie notes as she leads the way out to the deck. “Tara, your trainer, will be up in just a minute.”

Once Annie goes back inside, I give Mom the *look*, which she returns, and we shake our heads together. I appreciate that Mom lets me handle adults who don’t seem totally able to deal with my chair. It doesn’t mean we can’t roll our eyes about it after, though. Even in Iowa City, there was always the Walmart cashier or college student who seemed not to remember I was a functioning human being when they interacted with me.

But it’s easy to forget about Annie once I take in the view in front of me. The large deck overlooks a scattering of picnic tables, docks, and what must be the dolphin lagoon. Just beyond the lagoon is open water. A sheltered bench area in front of the dock obscures a complete view of the lagoon, but I can still see the far end and the gulf just past it. Unlike the beach on Sister Secret day, the water is a dark, dense blue. Not murky like Lake MacBride back in Iowa, but definitely not your classic Florida postcard.

Still, I feel like I’m in a Disney movie. The sky is a delightful shade of blue, I’m surrounded by radiant flowers, birds are chirping all around me, and I think I even saw a butterfly. The ocean (the ocean!) is right there, and even though I can’t see them yet, I’m closer than I’ve ever been to not one but *multiple* dolphins.

I literally pinch myself.

"Pretty cool, huh?" Mom asks, fixing her hat to block the sun from her face. Wynns don't joke around when it comes to UVA/UVB protection.

"I can't believe this is my reality right now."

"I'm glad you're happy," Mom says. She looks pretty happy, too. Her hair is a little wavier than usual, and I would never say this to her face, but the crinkles on the sides of her eyes when she smiles aren't as deep. Maybe it's the sunshine. Or maybe it's the close proximity to the world's most magical creatures (those creatures being dolphins).

I see Tara walking toward us from a building next to the docks. Unlike my encounter with Annie, just the sight of Tara immediately puts me at ease. She's like the camp counselor I never had, because, well, I've never been to camp. Her hair is also white-blond, but probably from the sun and not chemicals. As she nears, I see that light brown freckles dot almost every surface of her skin. She wears leggings, flip-flops, and a navy T-shirt with the Dolphina Cove logo. Solid dolphin trainer uniform. Around her neck, a silver whistle that reminds me of a squid hangs from a blue lanyard, glistening in the sun.

"Hi, I'm Tara! You must be KT," she says as she approaches. I meet her extended hand for a hearty shake. She looks me in the eye and smiles. "So excited to have you with us today!"

"Me, too!" I smile back without hesitation.

"So, here's the plan: I'll show you around a little bit, and then we'll get down to business. We'll spend the first part of our time together prepping for a training session so you can see what goes on behind the scenes. Then we'll get you in the water for a swim at the very end. How does that sound?"

"Great! The best! Let's do it!"

Hearing the words *in the water for a swim* makes it feel more real. My mind is moving a mile a minute. I have a gazillion questions and I also sort of want to tell Tara the tons of stuff I already know about dolphins.

"Tara, if it's okay, I'll let you guys do your thing while I get some work done here on the picnic tables," Mom says with a wink in my direction.

Mom is the best. Like Cady and Kaytee, she's good at reading my mind. I'm glad that the majority of this day will be all my own. Well, and Tara's. And ALL THE DOLPHINS I'M ABOUT TO MEET AND SWIM WITH AND BEFRIEND!

Nope, it hasn't gotten old yet.

"Absolutely, Mrs. Wynn. We'll make sure to grab you before the swim so you can watch and take pictures."

"And videos!"

"And videos," Mom assures me. "Have the best time, KT Lady."

With that, Tara and I chitchat as I follow her down a concrete path toward the dock.

"So, do you want to be a dolphin trainer one day?"

I think about it for a second. "I'm not sure." Honestly, I'd never considered it before. My main goal was just to find a way to hang out with them. "When did you know that's what you wanted to do?"

"I caught the dolphin bug when I was a little kid after a family trip to a sanctuary in Hawaii. I just thought they were so cool and wanted to learn everything I could about them."

"Totally! I visited the Chicago aquarium for the first time when I was in second grade and was instantly obsessed." I don't need to explain why. It feels pretty obvious to me why dolphins are the absolute best, and I'm 1,000 percent positive Tara gets it, too. "So you had to do all sorts of marine biology stuff in college?"

"Actually, I was a psychology major."

"No way! My mom's a psychology teacher! Um, I mean, professor." She'd kill me if she heard that mistake. Fair enough. She spent like a gazillion years in school to earn her professor title.

"Yeah, working with marine mammals is actually a lot about studying behavior and reading and interpreting actions." Tara pauses and turns to look back at me. "Watch that break in the sidewalk. Do you need help getting over it?" Tara asks, referring to what could only be described as a canyon in the cement.

"No thanks, I got it."

"Cool." Tara turns back around and continues down the path. I like Tara already. I give myself a wind-up wheel (that's a technical term meaning an extra effort of speed before an obstacle like a bump, hill, or, in this case, a sidewalk canyon, to make the maneuver more manageable) and glide over the crack, no problem.

"Anyway, as you'll see, most of the work we do with dolphins is about forming relationships, intuiting the animal's needs, and shaping their behavior in a positive way. We sort all their meals and feed them, but aren't the ones to determine their individualized dietary requirements, for example."

"Gotcha," I say. I can't wait to tell Mom that with everything she knows about psychology, she could be a professionally trained slash certified dolphin expert in no time. Maybe it runs in the family.

Once we arrive at the dock, I lock my wheels a few feet from the edge and peer into the dark water. The lagoon is smaller than a football field—no, smaller than half a football field, actually. To my left, another part of the dock juts into the water like a peninsula, perpendicular to the one we're on, serving as a pathway so trainers or visitors can access most of the lagoon, I guess. What looks like a short fence covered in shrubs and swampy weeds separates the outer edge of the lagoon from open water.

The same beautiful flowers from the parking lot line the perimeter. It's very tranquil. *Too* tranquil?

"Where are they?" I ask. I sense movement beneath the surface of the water, but can't see anything. Not yet. "Are they sleeping?" That's the only explanation I can think of. Or hiding.

"Oh no, they're just playing hard to get," Tara says, raising the volume of her voice as if she's talking both to me and all the invisible dolphins.

"How deep is this water?" I ask. I was expecting it to be crystal clear. Like the postcards and the pool at the Iowa City YMCA where I learned to swim.

"Oh, it's a good twenty feet. Plenty of depth for the animals to get enough exercise."

"What's down there?" I wonder aloud.

"Same as the ocean floor." I'm not familiar with the ocean floor. "Seaweed, plants. Open ocean water can come in and out of the lagoon with the tides, as well as fish."

"Fish are in the lagoon, too?" I strain to see. X-ray vision would be cool at a time like this.

"Sure. We want to maintain as organic an environment as possible for the animals. Because we feed them and reward their behavior with food, they rarely hunt, but there are fish for them to eat if they'd like. But they tend to get lazy."

Hunt is the main word that sticks out. I never thought of dolphins as hunters. Just adorable creatures that glide through aqua water and jump in the air with glee. This is different than what I imagined. Not necessarily less postcard-y. Maybe just a different postcard.

"Just over there"—Tara points to the hedge fence on the far end of the lagoon—"is the gulf. As I mentioned, small fish and marine life can come and go, so this space really mimics their natural habitat."

"Sweet."

"Let's see who's ready to play . . ." Tara looks around the lagoon. "Luna, Sammy, Ginger, don't be shy!"

Evidence of a slight current ripples the surface of the water, but no dolphins yet. I soften my focus so I can take in the entire lagoon at once. I have no idea where the first one will pop up, and I don't want to miss it.

And then it happens. A dorsal fin slices through the surface of the water the length of two Belugas in front of me. Then another.

They're so close!

"Luna, there you are, baby," Tara says in the tone one might use talking to a toddler. Except she's basically screaming, which somehow makes the cooing voice not annoying.

I let my eyes follow where I imagine Luna and the other fin

have swum. It seemed like they were circling back to the far end. I use my arms to push myself a little higher in my chair when it finally happens.

First, its nose and then its head burst through the surface. Just like in *Flipper* and every cartoon and movie combined, a dolphin bobs right in front of us, making that high-pitched clicking sound that I know for sure is laughing.

I, in turn, start to laugh uncontrollably. Like Luna is tickling my heart. Once I start, I can't stop. It's amazing.

"Luna, you are just the cutest, aren't you?" Tara exclaims, as if she, too, is seeing her for the first time. "Her daughter, Sammy, is usually right behind. They're still very attached— Oh, there she is!"

Another dolphin that basically looks like Luna but a tiny bit smaller swims up. A moment later they dip back underwater, tails making small splashes as they go.

"Oh, okay, Sammy, not being friendly today, I see." Tara laughs again. "I still love you!" She turns her attention back my way and resumes her talking-to-a-human voice. "We have seven dolphins living with us at Dolphina Cove right now. The youngest calf is about one, and the most mature female is almost thirteen."

"Like me!" I announce.

"Oh, cool, birthday coming up?"

"Forty-eight days," I answer. "Not that I'm counting . . ."

"Thirteenth birthday is big," Tara confirms. I couldn't agree more.

Tara continues to describe the characteristics of each dolphin. Ginger has a nick in her tail, and Luna was injured when they found her, and now has a cross-bite, though she doesn't seem to be in any pain. I do my best to listen and watch at the same time. Unlike when we first approached, the dolphins are more active now. Some come to us with their mouths open (hoping for food, Tara explains), while others seem to be taking their morning swim around the lagoon. Just when I least expect it, a new dolphin pops up to the surface. Dolphins could make great ninjas; they're really on point with stealth moves.

"We'll be back to play later, cuties," Tara coos. Then, to me, "We need to go sort and weigh the fish before the first session."

"Sounds good," I respond. I reach down to unlock my wheels when a flash of movement at the far end of the lagoon catches my eye.

If I were a cartoon character, my jaw would be on the floor. Literally. Tongue out like a red carpet. That's how incredible it is to see a dolphin jump into the air.

"Oh, Cola, you're such a show-off!" Tara exclaims. Cola leaps again, and then again, each time higher than the last.

"Wow." I'm surprised I could even get a syllable out. I'm

tempted to take a video with my phone. Cady and Kaytee—and, really, anyone with a bit of sense—would lose their minds if they saw this.

"Cola is our newest. Only been with us for a couple of weeks. He's a sweetie, but sure has a lot of energy."

Cola leaps again, then swims around the perimeter of the lagoon. His dorsal fin slices through the surface of the water. He dips completely under, only to resurface a moment later, cascading through the water. *I see you, Cola,* I think. I notice that all the other dolphins have retreated to their hiding places beneath the water's surface.

"Yep, quite the personality," Tara reiterates. Then, once more to Cola, "Show-off!"

Watching Cola, it strikes me: These animals are majestic. And strong. And graceful. And absolutely enormous. I feel like a little ant next to them. Good thing dolphins are also cute.

After the mini dolphin introduction, Tara takes me back to the trainers' office, which consists of a room with two computers, a smattering of folding chairs, a long plastic table, and a giant whiteboard. A doorway on the opposite side from where we entered reveals what seems to be a sort of kitchen but without a stove or oven for cooking. Gigantic metal countertops and sinks line the white walls, next to a row of three monstrous refrigerators. The whole room is covered in tile, reminding me of an empty swimming pool. Also, it smells like chlorine and fish. More fish than chlorine.

Okay, all fish.

"This is where we have our staff meetings, and where all the schedule and feeding information is kept." The phone rings. "One sec," Tara says as she goes to answer. "Trainers' office, this is Tara," I hear her say.

While she chats, I maneuver Sprinkle around the folding chairs to get a better look at the whiteboard. Each of the seven dolphins gets their own column with their picture next to their name like they're movie stars. Next to each dolphin headshot, in perfect, loopy handwriting, are reminders and lists of chemicals: *2.5L H2O *New eye drops* for Luna, *3L H20 Tacro w/ Ace, RL BD* for Sammy, and *Chlorex rinse mouth CAT* for Ginger.

Next to the technical slash science-y notes is a section for what seems to be more training-related details. *Luna: Don't ask for elephant UFN.* Cola has special instructions to *ask for 5–6 deep breaths in AM or PM.* Wow. It's as if they're humans. I wonder if deep breaths do the same thing for dolphins as for people. I had a teacher back in second grade who always told us to take a "balloon breath" if we were feeling angry or sad. Does Cola need that reminder in the morning or at night, too? I think about when I saw him swimming laps and leaping out of the water. He probably needs to catch his breath at the very least.

Below, Cola also has another note highlighted with red asterisks: *Only tail wave with guests.*

"So," Tara says when she's done on the phone, "as you can see, we keep things pretty detailed around here."

I nod. I can't help but wonder why Cola only tail waves. I also desperately want to see a tail wave. If I had a tail, I'd probably use it to wave all the time. Why not?

"I just talked to Annie up at the office. It's pretty mellow today; the only session with guests isn't until the end of the day." Then, slightly under her breath, "Annie has a heart of gold but is still learning the ropes. Anyway, it'll just be you and the trainers all morning."

"Great!" It didn't occur to me that there would be other visitors around during my time here. It is a fully operational dolphin sanctuary slash research center, after all. Duh.

Tara takes me to the kitchen-y space where the other two trainers on duty sort fish from big cardboard boxes into buckets that hang from hooks attached to some sort of scale that dangles from the ceiling.

"Y'all, this is KT, my shadow for the day. KT, this is Jolie and Natalia."

"Heyyy," they say in unison, peeking over their shoulders.

"I'd shake your hand, but I'm covered in half-frozen fish guts!" Natalia says cheerfully.

"Welcome, KT!" Jolie exclaims.

One thing I'm learning about dolphin trainers: They have no shortage of enthusiasm. Also, a major part of their job is sorting out fish and organizing all the fish into a gazillion different buckets. Much more to this dolphin-trainer thing than cuddling with gigantic marine mammals all day.

"Each dolphin gets a specialized diet," Tara says as she lifts a cardboard box onto the counter. She digs in and starts dropping half-frozen Pacific herring into metal buckets. They clank like icicle instruments. "Our girl Sammy needs a little more meat on her bones, so she'll get fattier fish than, say, Luna."

"What about Cola?" I ask.

"Sweet baby Cola is healthy as a horse," Tara says.

"Weird comparison, *Tar*," Jolie jokes.

"Psssh," Tara says, pretending to throw a sardine in Jolie's direction.

Tara, Natalia, and Jolie break down how the feeding works. The first task in the morning is always sorting food, which takes a while because dolphins eat a lot. Like twenty-five pounds of fish per day. That's like one and a half Sprinkles. Most of their fish comes frozen straight from Canada.

"And dolphins live until they're, like, thirty to fifty, right?" I can't help showing off what I've learned about dolphins over the years. I want Tara and all present company to know they're dealing with a pseudo-expert.

"Yep. Generally, they live much longer here with us than they would in the wild," Jolie says.

"Do the dolphins here ever go back into the wild?" I ask.

"No, not usually. In some scenarios, we might transfer one to a more suitable sanctuary, but once a dolphin has been under our care, it's not easy for them to transition back into open water. Mainly because they're not used to hunting."

Interesting.

Tara adds, "When I mention to people that I'm a dolphin trainer, they sometimes come at me with stereotypes, like, *Oh, you trap dolphins for a living?*"

I swallow, glad she can't read my mind. I remember when a similar fear crossed my brain.

"Or my favorite," Natalia says. "*Don't you feel bad keeping wild animals in a tank?*"

"*So* not a tank," Jolie confirms, gesturing with a fish-gutty finger toward the lagoon.

"So annoying," Natalia adds.

I know the feeling, I think but don't say.

Natalia spells it out. "Our sweet babies are fed well, cared for if they're sick or injured, and basically get dozens of belly rubs all day."

"In other words," Tara adds, "dolphins here at Dolphina Cove—or at any other sanctuary, for that matter—are really living their best lives."

Them and me both.

* * *

Over the next hour, I watch Tara weigh more buckets of fish, insert vitamins into the fish gills, and clean every surface with a special soap and drown everything in water. Finally, it's time for the playing part, aka a training session. My heart twirls with excitement.

A "session," I learn, is when trainers work with dolphins one-on-one to practice different behaviors. The whistles hanging around their necks are actually called *bridges*, which I personally think is much cooler than *whistle*. Mysterious, yet professional. Tara uses her bridge (or bridges) whenever Sammy does the behavior she asks, so the dolphin hears the high-pitched tweet and associates it with that behavior. With Tara, Jolie, and Natalia all in session at the same time, regular chirps fill the air.

I learn so much more from observing a session than I would from the Internet. First, dolphins have toys for days. Hula-hoops, balls of various sizes, and Frisbees. The trainers call these toys *enrichment*. Technical term. Playing with a pool noodle, Natalia explains between bridges, isn't just fun for the animals, but resembles movements and challenges the dolphins might experience in the wild, which keeps them both mentally and physically fit. Pretty cool. The ultimate two birds, one stone situation.

Second, all successful completions of a behavior are rewarded with positive reinforcement of a fish, a fish frozen in a block of ice, or flavorless Jell-O. Tara lets me throw a reinforcement (a hunk of Jell-O) to Sammy when she successfully retrieves a piece of enrichment (a red buoy). Fun fact that even I was unaware of, despite my dolphin obsession: Dolphins don't chew their food. That's right. They have tons of little Tic Tac teeth, but those are only used to snag the goods. Once food is in their possession, they just swallow it whole, like that time Dad tried to teach Lucy and me how to eat oysters (shellfish in Iowa? Um, no thank you).

Third, not that this is really news per se, but wow can dolphins get air. Sammy (yes, Sammy, the youngest dolphin in the lagoon) can essentially do the dolphin equivalent of a dunk. She's able to launch herself out of the water like an actual torpedo. I can't help but laugh uncontrollably when I see her—it's just so amazing!—but part of me wonders if she could leap over a house. Like a two-story house. I look at the barrier of shrubs that separates the lagoon from open water.

"Could she jump over that fence thing?" I ask Tara.

"Oh, yeah, if she wanted to." Then, to Sammy, "Couldn't you, big girl?"

"Shouldn't the fence be a little higher, then?"

"Dolphins are extremely powerful animals. But they don't have depth perception, so they can't actually see that they're easily able to hop the fence."

Tara goes on to explain that dolphins see out of each eye separately. Very cool, and makes me dizzy to think about. They also only sleep with half of their brain at a time, so one half of their brain is active while the opposite eye stays open and alert. Humans are involuntary breathers (we can breathe even when we're sleeping, without thinking about it), but dolphins are not, which is why they have to stay half-awake all the time. Thinking about that kind of makes my whole brain tired. I don't totally get it, but it sounds like something every kid under the age of eighteen would love to be able to do.

Tara takes more time to confirm that while this might seem like boot camp (definitely not what I was thinking, but she has a point), dolphins are extremely intelligent and curious creatures. Sessions are actually really fun and stimulating for them. As an extremely intelligent and curious creature myself, I hope seventh grade at Fernbank Middle School, which begins in less than twenty-four hours, feels the same way.

While Tara works with Sammy on a behavior only slightly less dramatic than Olympic gymnastics, I watch Natalia and Cola. Cola is definitely active and splashy.

"Is Cola going to practice his tail flip?" I ask, remembering the note on the whiteboard. I don't want Cola to miss out on all the fun.

"Right now, we're just working on bonding," Natalia says. "Isn't that right?" Natalia tweets her bridge and throws Cola a slightly bloody fish. He gobbles it up and dives underneath the water.

Natalia tweets her bridge once, and then again, but Cola doesn't return.

"Cola away," she announces. She must see the concern on my face because she explains, "That just means I've lost sight of him, and it lets the other trainers know. It's all about communication over here."

A moment later, Cola appears with a shameless grin on his face, mouth open, smiling big, apparently ready for more treats. Or more fun. Or both.

Toward the end of the session, after Cola completes a particularly impressive aerial move, Natalia bridges and he glides over for a belly rub. Natalia lies on her stomach on the deck and reaches her hand to graze Cola's white underside.

"Good job, Cola! You know I love you so much."

Cola looks quite pleased with himself. Though I'm only several feet away, I'm not sure if he can see me, but I give him a solid grin and a wave anyhow. Then—and I swear this is true—Cola lifts his right fin and waves right back! It's a Dolphina Cove miracle! Unfortunately, the impromptu wave also splashes Natalia right in the face.

"Bad manners, Cola," she scolds. "You know better." Cola swims away, slipping his tail up for another splash before he disappears.

He does not get a fish or Jell-O when he returns a moment later.

Chapter 6

Finally, it's time for the main event. The big swim. I, KT Wynn—twelve, almost thirteen, Iowa City native, lifelong Libra, crayon doodler extraordinaire, future award-winning journalist, rocky road ice cream enthusiast—am about to swim with a real, live dolphin. I actually can't believe it.

I also can't totally believe how many people showed up. After spending most of the day alone with Tara, Natalia, and Jolie (though Annie popped her head in a few times, too), I had forgotten that other guests would be joining us for a dolphin encounter of their very own. I was slightly disappointed to see the parking lot begin to fill up with cars. This whole experience has been so private, and I'm not sure if I want to share it. Not that I have a choice.

By the time I've changed into my bathing suit, the other guests are crowded behind the trainers' office. As I near, I see they're in line getting fitted for life jackets. When it's my turn, Jolie sizes me up and hands me what looks like a life jacket for, well, a dolphin. It's gigantic.

"I think it may be a little big," I say.

"You don't want it too tight," she explains.

I put my arms through the vest and snap the three front buckles. The shoulders ride up to my ears.

"Are you sure I won't, like, slip out?"

"Not a chance."

I try to trust her. She's a professional. She knows. *I'm a strong swimmer, anyway,* I remind myself. It's not like I'd drown if the life vest were to float away without me inside.

When life jackets are secured, Jolie leads everyone down to the dock. I didn't notice this before, but a rectangular piece of the dock right in front of the picnic benches operates like an elevator. Tara explains to the crowd that when it's our turn, we'll get on it and then be lowered into the water. Convenient, I guess. It also reminds me of this part in a horror movie that Cady made me watch last Halloween that I can't remember the name of. Weird.

Tara says I'm up first. "VIP," she whispers with a wink.

I give her a thumbs-up because suddenly my chest feels too fluttery to talk. Mom helps me move from Sprinkle into a floating chair provided by Dolphina Cove. She's made of big white PVC pipes that remind me of the dentist for some reason. If she had a name (I'm not sure if she's worthy of a name), it would be Boodles or something equally unpleasant to say out loud. Once I'm in, Mom pushes me onto the elevator dock next to Tara.

Mom leans down to whisper, "Do you want me to come with you?" so nobody else can hear.

I shake my head.

"I'll get it all filmed for you." Mom squeezes my shoulder, and then it's just Tara and me.

Because that butterfly feeling in my chest is growing stronger, and this bubbling chair makes me feel smaller, I remind myself that it will be fine. I love dolphins. The trainers love dolphins. The dolphins are living their best lives here at Dolphina Cove. It's all fine. I love dolphins and it's all fine.

Tara gives a wave to Natalia, who then pushes a button. We lower into the water at a comically slow pace. Surprisingly, the elevator dock doesn't make any cranking sounds as we descend. The other guests watch from the stationary docks. There are about two dozen of them in total. Some are young kids, and there's one other teenager who looks super bored. Most of them are sunburned; probably tourists.

But I'm a local now.

I hear faint sniffling behind me. I turn and see a girl who looks to be around five. Her hair is long and tangled, and her striped red-and-white one-piece bathing suit is extremely cute. She hides her face in her dad's shoulder.

"Don't worry, baby, the dolphins are nice." The girl buries her face deeper into his armpit. "Look, she's doing it. Look how brave she is. You can be just as brave as her!" The girl peeks one eye out and looks my way. I give her a little wave. She blinks back at me with big, quivering eyes. *I feel you,* I want to say.

I'm snapped back to reality once I'm waist deep and can feel how cold the water is. And yes, the water is still murky while I'm in it. I'm submerged to my chest, and I can hardly see my lap when I look down. It's also colder than I expected or remembered from the stray splashes I felt on my arms during the training session.

This is the first time I've been in the ocean. I immediately miss the over-chlorinated pools I'm familiar with.

The dock stops moving. Or sinking, rather. Here we go.

"First, Sammy is going to join us so you can get a touch, and then we'll unbuckle you so you can swim out and get a ride and a kiss."

I nod.

"Okay, hold out your hands in front of you, like this." Tara demonstrates. I mimic her, so my hands are in front of me like a zombie. I'm very cold now. I wish the sun were closer to the earth. I don't see Sammy anywhere.

"Just keep them right there."

Tara bridges and Sammy magically appears in front of us.

"There you go, Sammy. Now, KT, just keep your hands right there for a shake."

Sammy faces me square on and literally puts her fins in my waiting hands. Which is cool. For sure cool. I can now confirm that dolphin skin feels exactly how I imagined and also not at all like it. Like rubber and windbreaker material had a monstrous, whale-sized baby.

Yes, Sammy is huge. Her size up close proves more impressive than her skin.

I shiver.

"Perfect. Thank you, Sammy. You're such a good girl!" Tara throws Sammy a fish. Sure enough, she uses her Tic Tac teeth to snag the little guy. There sure are a lot of them. Probably more than she needs. Great hunting teeth. Could definitely bite if they wanted to. Sammy swims away, and though her tail doesn't smack me in the face, I flinch anyway. Her change of direction causes a swell and the water suddenly rises to my chin.

I can't help but imagine everything that's beneath the surface of the water. Seven dolphins. Some innocent fish that may be eaten by the aforementioned dolphins. Seaweed. Maybe some crabs. Possibly an eel. Shoot, there could be the remains of a shipwreck for all I know.

And me.

Tara instructs me to unbuckle from the chair. When I do, I float to the surface of the water. The life jacket that I knew was a little too big doesn't slide off me, but it is super uncomfortable. It digs into the bottoms of my armpits. I don't even need it. I haven't swum with a life jacket in years, and it makes me feel wobbly, when usually in the water I feel like a mermaid because it's the only place I can move freely without fighting gravity.

"Okay, when I say so in a minute, you can swim out to the middle of the lagoon. We'll start with a dorsal pull first, and then go for a little kiss!" Tara howls. "Once you've swum out, all you'll need to do is hold your hands out like you did before for the shake. When Sammy swims by, grab on to her top fin, and she'll give you a little ride back into the dock."

At least I think that's what she said. Maybe she said more, I'm not sure. It's hard to pay attention when I'm so cold and shivery and my chest feels so fluttery, and my stomach, too, now that I think about it. I know Sammy's swimming around below me somewhere, but I can't see her. I imagine her charging back and forth. And then I imagine Luna and Cola and Ginger and the three others all doing the same thing. A lagoon full of charging, toothy dolphins nowhere actually to be seen.

Oh, boy. I could puke, I think. If I puke, will the dolphins be grossed out?

"Sammy away!" Tara's lost sight of her. Sammy could be anywhere. Across the lagoon, right next to me, right under me about to shoot up. If dolphins don't have depth perception, how on earth will they avoid smacking into me?

I suddenly wish I were swimming with Cola. Even though he's new to Dolphina Cove, dolphin training is all about relationships, right? We had a moment. A wave. Cola gets me. Right?

Sammy is still away, and most of the dolphins are doing that thing where they're hiding again. A dorsal fin or tail here and there, but the more I consider what's really occurring, it feels like chaos, and I have no idea what could happen next. Why does the water have to be so not transparent? How is this the one place in all of postcard-y Florida with dangerous dark water, like it's hiding a secret?

I sense movement again. Sammy's back at the dock, next to Tara. She feeds her a fish. I realize how far I've floated from the dock. I could easily swim back, but suddenly I feel all alone out here. KT Island in the dolphin lagoon.

I glance at my mom, who gives me a wave. All the other guests lean on the dock railing, watching the scene unfold. I'm in the spotlight.

"Good girl, Sammy. You're doing so great, aren't you?" Tara coos. "Okay, KT, now put your hands up in front of you like before."

I'm about to, but the image of six more dolphins runs on a loop in my mind. Six more dolphins that I can't see. Six more dolphins without depth perception charging underwater with Tic Tac teeth that can snag fish—or an almost-thirteen-year-old girl bobbing helplessly in the middle of a murky lagoon.

I think about bridging, and how it literally makes no sense that a human can communicate with an animal with a single whistle sound.

I think about dolphins being gigantic, oversized marine mammals.

I think about the times during training that Sammy and Ginger and Luna and the others didn't earn a reinforcement, and how Cola's only trained to tail wave with guests.

How do the trainers *really* know what is going to happen?

I steal a glance up, away from the maybe-eel-maybe-monster-infested mystery water. The sky is still Disney-movie blue, which feels strangely optimistic in this moment. Mocking, really.

I try to lift my arms, and as Sammy swims by, some salt water seeps into my mouth. It tastes almost poisonous. Sammy dashes by. Like a torpedo, a bullet, a predator. There's no way I could've caught her dorsal fin even if I'd wanted to. And I'm not sure I want to anymore. The pressure of her wake confirms that she is big and I am small and—

I have to get out of here.

"Sammy away. Cola away," Natalia calls from her station on the dock.

Tara bridges, I think. Then she slaps the water with the palm of her hand. The sound cracks like a whip.

I have to get out of here right now.

"Tara, I'm actually really nauseous," I cry. "I'm gonna barf."

Or maybe I didn't say that at all. I certainly meant to. I mainly remember swimming as fast as possible back to the closest dock. Not the movable one, just the closest way to get out of the water. There was a lot of splashing. Swimming with a life vest is much harder than regular swimming.

As Mom and Natalia lift me out of the water and onto the dock, all I can imagine is dozens of Tic Tac teeth nipping at my toes. When I'm out, I frantically look to find my feet to make sure they're not bleeding without my knowledge. I spend the next forty-five minutes seated safely in Sprinkle, wrapped tight in a towel, watching the other guests get dorsal pulls and kisses from the dolphins. The entire time Mom gently strokes the wet ponytail plastered to my neck. Tara asks if I want to give it another go at the end of the session, but I shake my head no.

I'm never, ever getting back in that water.

* * *

At the end of the day, I give Tara and the other trainers hugs goodbye. I assure them that, yes, I'm totally fine, no big deal, must have gotten seasick, had the best day ever. They look a little worried still, but I insist I'm fine. I keep on insisting until their smiles look a little more relaxed and the flood of worry has left their eyes, though my chest still feels a little fluttery. I'm pretty sure that by the end they believe my lie. Maybe it wasn't a lie. Maybe I really was seasick.

No. It was the water. The unpredictability. The size. Surprises nonstop.

Tigers are cool, but I don't want to go in a cage with them.

Sammy never gave me a kiss. I never got to ride on her dorsal fin, never sailed through the water like the kids with the big smiles in all the photos.

That little girl in the striped one-piece probably didn't think I was brave at all.

I leave Dolphina Cove sad, scared, disappointed, and ashamed. Too many emotions for one almost-thirteen-year-old girl at once.

I tell Mom I don't want to talk about it on the way home. All I can think about, as warm air filters through the open window and palm trees make long shadows over the road in the afternoon sun, is how much I miss snow.

* * *

I only check my phone when I'm at home, in my bedroom that I don't share with Lucy, door shut. I have a bazillion texts from Cady and Kaytee asking for pictures and updates and more pictures.

Nothing about today makes sense. How can some of the best moments of your life be followed by some of the worst? I don't understand how the thing I love the most can also be the scariest.

Dolphins are supposed to be fun and playful and joyful and happy and wonderful. They're supposed to bring joy and laughter. They *do* bring joy and laughter. Why not to me? Why not anymore?

Iowa City feels farther away than ever.

Dad comes into my bedroom to say good night. His leather-bound journal is in his hand.

"Write anything good?"

Dad went to school for poetry. He realized halfway through his master's degree that there was no way he'd make a living doing it, so he tagged along with a friend on a residential electrician gig, and it became his day job. Then it became his job-job.

He takes a big breath and lets it out slowly. I like how Dad thinks about his answers, doesn't just say them. "The air is different here," he says finally.

"That's not the only thing," I mutter.

"Different air, different words."

I nod. Though what he said basically makes no sense, I think I get it. I'm glad I'm not the only one who might feel like they're suddenly living in outer space.

"How are you doing, KT Lady?"

"I'm fine," I respond quickly.

"Mom told me today ended a little differently than you expected." *Different.* The word of the day, week, and probably year.

I nod again. Now that I'm not near the potentially

eel-infested dangerous water and hypothetically menacing marine mammals, my fear of swimming with my still-beloved dolphins feels a little less severe.

"You don't look totally fine."

I shrug. I'm not sure what will happen to my voice if I try to speak. I could cry, and after the long day in the sun, I'm just not in the mood.

"Remember: If something doesn't feel doable, you'll just find another way to make it happen." He looks me in the eye for a few seconds, then adds, "But only if you want to. Okay?"

"Okay," I acknowledge.

Dad kisses me good night on my forehead, just to the right of center like always.

"Leave the door open," I remind him when he turns to go.

"Of course. For the ghosts to sneak out," he replies, referring to a longstanding Wynn family joke that nobody really remembers the origin of anymore. Yes, tradition is tradition. Some things aren't meant to change.

I send Cady and Kaytee some stills from the Dolphina Cove parking lot and text, **More to come!** before turning my phone on silent.

But not before I set my alarm. Tomorrow is the first day of school.

Chapter 7

I awake to the smell of muffins of the blueberry-cornflake variety. When I open my eyes, I'm temporarily disoriented. The room is dark, but the walls are bare. My dresser isn't by the doorway, it's next to my bed, the window faces the wrong way, and nobody is snoring in the top bunk.

Oh, right. I'm in Florida. Not home. Those muffins, though . . .

Dad makes blueberry-cornflake muffins every time there's a big day ahead. A "big day" can be a birthday (forty-seven days, by the way), the first day of the NCAA basketball tournament, or if he had a happy dream the night before. One morning in May, I came into the kitchen and he threw a warm muffin to me before declaring, "Happy Rainy Monday Appreciation Day!" (For the record, it was hardly even drizzling, but ever since the beginning of the week, precipitation feels like good luck.) Whatever the occasion, made-up or legit, Dad always determines when there's a big day. And, historically, the first day of school counts as a big day. He must have gotten up extra, extra early to make them before he had to leave for work.

It's still dark outside, so it's really the muffins that get me out of bed, not the promise of daylight. I can only snooze so long when there is such a delicious scent in the air. I was tossing and turning all night anyway. The first day of school is always nerve-racking, but if the first day of seventh grade—in a new school—were an earthquake, it'd measure off the charts on the Richter scale.

I grab a muffin from the kitchen and bring it back to the bathroom to nibble on while I get the flat iron going. I'm not going to deal with this Southern frizz on day one.

The muffins are good, but—and I'd never tell Dad this—they tasted better back in Iowa City. Maybe it's the water here or something. Kaytee once told me that bagels can only truly be made in New York because there's some special mineral in their tap water that adds a unique flavor. Maybe that's the case for Iowa City and blueberry-cornflake muffins.

One hour later, I examine myself in the mirror. Not bad. I'm wearing a lavender cap-sleeve T-shirt I got at the mall before we moved, white jean shorts, and a pair of white low-top Converse. An outfit that really says, "Iowa flair, don't care, ready to rock, ready to roll . . ." I haven't figured out the rest. On second thought . . .

"Luce, will you come here for last looks?" I call. I make sure my dolphin studs are locked in extra tight. They fit perfectly on my slightly-smaller-than-typical earlobes.

“Don’t be lazy. Come in here,” she answers.

Ugh, fine, I think. Lucy doesn’t let me get away with anything, which is annoying but also a very important quality in a sister.

I wheel into Lucy’s room to get an outfit check. She sits on her bed, cross-legged, French braiding her hair.

“When’d you learn that?” I ask.

“I dunno.” Never in the history of Lucy Wynn has she worn her honeycomb-blond (what some might call dirty blond but, no, because—rude) hair in anything other than a topknot or ponytail. I mean, *never*. Even when she’s fresh out of the shower, it always goes right up.

“Cute,” I say. It is, though it’s amazing how different someone you’ve known your whole life can look with a slightly changed hairdo. “My first-day outfit on point?”

“Solid,” Lucy says.

“I picked the lavender top because I think it accentuates my tan,” I explain. Sun-kissed skin seems like the right first-day-of-Florida-school vibe. “But I also have the coral one with the V-neck and tiny pocket.”

“Lavender for life,” Lucy says definitively. “Ugh, this is so hard,” Lucy mutters to herself. She messes up her hair to start over.

"You snooze, you lose on the muffins," I say. "You know I'm a bottomless pit when it comes to breakfast carbs."

"True story. I'll be out in a sec," Lucy answers. I turn Sprinkle to go, when she adds, "Hey. Fernbank Middle School won't know what hit 'em. Let's have a great day. Sister Secret."

"Sister Secret."

And even though it's more of a promise than a secret, I feel better knowing that Lucy and I are on the same page. New grade, new school, new state, new looks, and new Sister Secrets.

Off we go.

Chapter 8

The first thing that strikes me about Fernbank Middle School is the teal. So. Much. Teal. It's a pretty color, and I know, I know, we're near the ocean, and I get it's the school's color (well, teal and gray, technically, but the gray doesn't exactly pop), but my goodness, it's everywhere: the sign that says "Fernbank Middle School, Learning Today, Leading Tomorrow!" outside the main entrance. The front doors. The trim below the roof of the low buildings. The poles that hold up the awnings lining the hallways. The lockers. The general vibe. Aquatic overkill. Like the humidity, it's relentless. Iowa City Middle School's colors were black and yellow, but it's not like everything was painted like a bumblebee.

Oh! And the hallways aren't inside. That's right. The passageways connecting classrooms, cafeteria, and the main office are open-air. A (teal) roof thing keeps everything covered, but there are no walls. They're like wall-less hallways. It's all very Florida. This kind of architecture would never fly in Iowa City; it gets way too cold and snowy.

As planned, Mom comes into school early with me so we can touch base with the principal and make sure cutout desks are set up in my classrooms, the elevator between floors is working, there's a plan in place for gym, et cetera, et cetera; stuff that happened when I started middle school last year in Iowa City but wasn't all that complicated because Principal Boundy and my mom went to high school together, and she's known me since I was born, so she was super cool and on top of everything.

"So happy to have you joining us here at Fernbank Middle," Principal Lim says after we've gone over all the details. "I know it's tough to adjust to a new state and a new school. If you need anything, my door is always open." She looks me in the eye when she speaks to me. Phew.

"Thanks," I say, and mean it.

Principal Lim turns to Mom. "Same goes for you, Mrs. Wynn."

I hear a timid knock on the door. When I turn to see who's there, a head with lots of short, dark brown braids, wide brown eyes, and jittery eyebrows appears in the doorway. The girl's body is hidden behind the wall, her head floating in the air like a balloon without a string.

"Sabina, perfect timing," Principal Lim says. "You can come on in.

Sabina walks through the door. She wears cuffed jeans and

a yellow-and-white-striped T-shirt. She holds the shoulder straps of her backpack tight in her hands and taps her right foot to a nonexistent beat. She also smiles big, revealing perfect teeth behind a very obvious retainer.

I have always been a fan of big smiles, retainers notwithstanding.

"Hey, I'm Sabina," she says with a little wave. "But everyone calls me Socks."

I instantly stare at her ankles. No socks in sight.

"Hi. I'm KT." I give her a wave that turns into a peace sign that then turns back into a wave, because I've never given anyone a peace sign before in my life, and that's just odd. Oof. Awkward. Socks doesn't seem thrown, though. I realize that for all she knows, this is my signature wave. She's never seen me wave before!

"Socks volunteered to show you around today," Principal Lim says. I like that she calls Sabina by her nickname. "Y'all have homeroom and a lot of your classes together. Plus, Socks is kind of like the mayor of this school."

I'm not sure what that means, but Socks takes a grand bow, which makes me grin. I notice her cheeks are slightly flushed when she's returned upright. She fiddles with one of her braids like it's a good luck charm.

"Dad will pick you up after school, okay?" Mom says.

"Okay." I'm relieved their schedules worked out so I don't have to take the bus. Mom's classes are all in the afternoon and evenings this semester, and Dad's job starts super early in the morning, so he's off just in time to get me by the last bell at two forty-five.

Mom gives me a hug and a sweet tug on a strand of my flat-ironed, frizz-less hair. "Have the best day, KT Lady."

Mom leaves, Principal Lim stays, and I follow Socks out to the Fernbank Middle hallways en route to homeroom. She walks, I wheel, and we talk. The nice thing about no walls is that the acoustics are better. It's actually easier to have a conversation than in the echoey corridors of Iowa City Middle.

Good thing, too, because Socks barely pauses for a breath.

"So we have almost every class together, except for math because I think you're advanced." Socks pauses to glance down at the schedule in my hand. "Yep, you have advanced math, but other than that we have everything together. Not that that's why I'm your buddy. I was way into it, but it doesn't hurt that our schedules are major simpatico, ya know?" she asks, and I nod. "It looks like your locker is in hall C, so we can hit that later."

Socks officially talks faster than anyone I have ever met. It's like her mouth has a motor.

"So this is the main hall. I mean, duh. The school is shaped like an E, so it's pretty easy in that sense."

I can already tell that the lack of walls on the hallways will be disorienting.

"Whatever you do," Socks continues, "don't go to the end of hall A before lunch, like no matter what, because that bathroom smells like rotten Cheerios before noon. It's unbearable, and I wouldn't want that kind of torture for you. Trust me. I learned the hard way."

Hallway 4 in Iowa City Middle always smelled like microwaved cat litter.

"Gotcha," I acknowledge. I look around, taking it all in, ignoring all the kids' eyes who linger on me a moment too long, then dart away when I make eye contact. I make sure to smile and act like I'm having a good time, because nobody wants to see a mopey girl in a chair.

A joke.

Sort of.

Not ready to try that one out loud.

"Sorry, I talk a lot when I'm nervous. Not that I'm nervous. I also talk a lot when I'm not nervous. I'm a talker!" Socks throws her hands up like she has no choice in the matter, which is probably true.

"All good," I say. I'm happy to have a talker as my official Fernbank Middle tour guide. "So, you're the mayor?"

"Unofficially, but basically officially," she declares proudly.

"My mom calls me a social butterfly. My brother, who's totally annoying, calls me a social carnivore. I think of myself as a social avocado: delicious, nutritious, and adaptable!"

"I'm into that vibe," I say. "Never met a social avocado before."

Socks suddenly stops moving. "Am I, like, walking too fast for you?"

"Nope, all good," I assure her.

"Oh, okay, cool. I don't want to be, um, weird or anything." Socks darts her eyes around like she's trying to spot a bee. "Anyway, I'm so rude! I haven't really even introduced myself. A little bit about me: I'm a Florida lifer, born and raised right here in Fernbank. I'm going out for basketball this year, but only if it's confirmed that I don't have to get braces again. I'm basically allergic to gluten and peanuts, but what I lack in wheat I make up for with sucrose!" Socks pops a handful of M&M's straight from her pocket into her mouth. "Blue ones are my favorite. My parents think I'm hyper."

Socks gives me a huge, closed-lip smile, two thumbs up, and keeps going.

We get to the doorway from the hallway to the stairwell. The elevator is right on the other side.

"Can you grab the door?" I ask once I see that it's one of the heavier steel ones that are a pain in the you-know-what to deal with on my own. Also, it's teal. Obviously.

"Oh, gosh, of course, so sorry!" Socks appears panic-stricken.

"Totally chill."

Socks holds the door open, and I cruise through. I press the button twice but it doesn't light up. Hopefully the elevator works. Students scamper up the stairs behind us. Hearing snippets of excited conversation, laughter, and shouts of greeting reminds me of the first-day-of-school whirlwind I'd be a part of at Iowa City Middle if I were there. I try not to think about it.

We wait for a moment in silence. Socks taps her foot against the linoleum floor and hums a song to herself. I think she wants to talk but doesn't know what to say. I got this.

"I'll ask for help if I need it," I add. "Like with doors and stuff."

"Okay."

"And you can ask me a question if you don't know what to do."

"Okay."

"Or even if you just have a question. I'd rather you ask."

"Okay. Don't have any. All good."

I hear the gears of the elevator moving behind the elevator doors, but they must be rusty. Sure is taking a while.

"Okay, I have one. Is that okay?" Socks spits out.

"Yep."

"Have you always used a wheelchair?"

"Pretty much."

"Like, you were born in one?"

"That's two questions. Over the limit." I couldn't resist.

"Oh, gosh, sorry, I—"

"Kidding, kidding, I promise!"

Socks plays with a braid sprouting from her temple, but she keeps her eyes on me. For a talker, she's way above average at eye contact.

"I was in an accident when I was really young, so basically my whole life. I don't know it any other way."

At last, the elevator arrives, and we go inside. I press the button for the second floor and the lift makes its slow trek up. Like, turtle slow. It reminds me of being lowered into the dolphin-infested lagoon.

It's been at least three seconds, and Socks hasn't made a peep. Although I've only known her for all of five minutes, I'm under the impression this pause in conversation (or monologue, if I'm being honest) is unusual for her.

"I've never been in this elevator before. Way off-limits," Socks whispers, as if we could get caught at any second.

"Stick with me, kid," I say with a dramatic wink, quoting a movie I forget the name of.

Socks laughs and lets out a breath I don't think either of us realized she'd been holding.

We finally arrive on the second floor and join the throngs of kids rushing to class.

"Ms. Vasquez's homeroom is down here to the right. Whatever you do, don't use the water fountain outside her room because it tastes kind of like chlorine and licorice. Nasty."

"We had a water fountain in Iowa City that tasted like bubble gum. Not as great as it sounds."

Socks makes a face. "Oh, and really important—"

But she stops speaking mid-sentence. I follow her gaze and my eyes land on a boy in a red hoodie leaning against a locker. I can smell his cologne already. I'm almost certain he stole it from an older brother. For someone living by the beach, he's very pale. And very tall.

"Hey, EJ!" Socks says.

"Yo," he grunts.

After we've passed, Socks whispers, "So EJ is best friends with Ayden, who's like childhood friends and also sort of best friends with Juan Carlos. You've haven't met them yet, but you will. I think EJ's cute or whatever, but that's it. I'm so busy with school and clubs and me time that we'll just be friends. Oh, here we are. Room 215. Homeroom, here we come!"

Socks holds the door open and I roll myself through. The classroom is cluttered—much more crowded than my sixth-grade homeroom. The teacher's desk is in the back of the room, not the front, which seems strange to me, but maybe I'm just not used to it.

I see my desk immediately. I'm relieved that Principal Lim was good on her word and they actually have my cutout desk, but I still hate that I need it. It's lower and bigger than all the other desks. Like someone doing the wrong choreography in a synchronized dance.

Straight out of the first-day-of-school handbook, Ms. Vasquez has us go around the room for a little icebreaker. "Team bonding," she calls it. "Everyone share their name and one thing you'd like us to know about you."

As my turn nears, I debate the perfect reveal. This is my first impression, after all, and I don't want to blow it. Nobody knows anything about me so the options are quite endless.

"KT Wynn, that's you, right?" Ms. Vasquez asks. All eyes are on me. I must have zoned out. Shoot. I hope it wasn't for long.

"Yep. Hi. Hey. I'm KT. I just moved here from Iowa City. I was offered an arm-wrestling scholarship for a school in the Swiss Alps, but I decided to come to Fernbank Middle because I'm obsessed with the color teal."

That gets a bigger laugh than I expected. Even Ms. Vasquez cracks a smile.

Then I add, "Iowa City is the best place ever." I speak so softly I'm not sure anyone can hear, but the words felt too important to keep in. I think about Kaytee and Cady and wonder how their first day of school is going.

I've never felt so homesick.

* * *

Morning passes quickly. The classrooms continue to be cramped and cold. I'm grateful for the outdoor hallways. Inside, the AC is set to what has to be polar level. I wish I had brought a blanket. Seriously. Shiver central.

Finally, it's lunch. Socks does not slack on her new-student-buddy duties. On our way to the cafeteria, she provides bits of information about the student body.

"Those are the twins that nobody can tell apart," she says, pointing to two very identical-looking boys. "And over there, Ava and Charlie"—a tall girl and a short boy hold hands as they talk closely in front of an open locker—"have been a couple since last year. Longest in our grade, for sure."

"We had a couple like that in Iowa City." I laugh to myself remembering the hallway drama when Isaiah asked Ruwa out with the assistance of a kazoo and top hat. "It's a long story," I assure Socks.

"Chill," she responds, though I'm a little disappointed she doesn't ask for the short version.

Socks continues to talk my ear off on the way to lunch. She's deep into a story about the time there was this big misunderstanding about Halloween costume dress code at school. Once she mentions food coloring and corn syrup, I start to zone out a bit, mind drifting to the Cruella de Vil and dalmatian costumes Cady, Kaytee, and I wore to school in fifth grade. We really knocked those out of the park. Socks slows down as we come to a girl with long braids that have a couple streaks of electric blue woven throughout.

"That's my cousin Jas," Socks whispers. She whispers when she's nervous about something, I realize. "Second cousin, technically, but still cousins."

Socks takes a step forward and taps Jas on the shoulder. She's putting some sort of sticker behind a little mirror for the back of her locker.

"Hey, Jas, this is KT. She's new," Socks offers by way of introduction.

"Nice to meet you, Jas," I say. "Sweet Converse." The whole footwear ensemble is pretty sweet, really. Her shoes are bright red with purple shoelaces. Not a combination you see often. "I'm dying for a pair of green ones. One of the downsides of Iowa City. Colorful-sneaker-shopping options so not on point."

Maybe I talk a lot, too, when I'm nervous. I sense Socks stiffen next to me.

"Well, there's always the Internet," Jas replies.

"Sure, but with sizing . . . you know." My mind races to find something else to say. "The Internet is chill, too, though."

"Nice to meet you," Jas says, though based on the look on her face, her experience of our exchange was anything but nice. She shuts her locker, and as she walks away, she scoffs, "Really, Socks?"

Once Jas is out of earshot, I ask, "Did I say something wrong?"

"Okay, so, how do I put it?" Socks seems flustered. I'm starting to realize that might just be her standard operating mode. "So, back in fourth grade, Jas begged her mom, who is my mom's first cousin, to get her a pair of green Converse, and she was so excited when she finally did that she wore them to school like every day for a month. Until finally one day Ayden said, 'Those are the color of boogers,' like really loud at recess, and it embarrassed Jas so much that she never, ever wore them again." Socks finally pauses to catch a breath. "Anyway, it got really nasty on Saint Patrick's Day that year. All I can say is, D-R-A-M-A."

I don't totally get it. "Is she still upset about it all these years later?"

"Hashtag duh! Jas has been in love with Ayden since third grade!" Socks exclaims like it's the most obvious thing in the world. Then, in a whisper, "That's, like, common knowledge!"

"Gotcha." But I still don't understand. Guess you had to be there. Licorice-infested water fountains, rotten Cheerios, and fourth-grade sneaker drama-trauma. As the new kid, I have a lot to catch up on. "Is that somehow related to how you got your nickname?" I've been waiting to ask her that since she (literally) popped her head into Principal Lim's office.

"Nickname, lifestyle, same difference. But no. I'm just a sock fanatic. Always have been, always will be."

I check her feet again. Nope. No socks in sight.

"I know what you're thinking. I'm wearing my lucky ones, duh, for the first day of school. They're ankle socks. The bottom looks like a shark's mouth and there are eyes on the toes."

"They should do that for a dolphin," I say, remembering how many tiny Tic Tac teeth Sammy revealed the other day.

"I'd buy them," Socks confirms. "Anyway, we should hustle so we can beat Jas and Kisa to the cafeteria. We don't want to get stuck at the tundra end of our table."

Apparently, the tundra end of the table is the one closest to the AC vent. Meaning it feels like a frozen tundra. As I've felt borderline hypothermic all day, I'm glad that there's still room on the tropical side when we arrive.

I'm also glad that I have people to eat lunch with. I've seen all the movies about new kids eating in a bathroom stall on the first day of school. I'm not trying to eat a peanut butter and jelly in the same place I pee, thank you very much.

I've never been timid in conversation. I'm not sure if that's the same thing as being shy, but I don't get that, either. Lucy tried to explain it to me once, but it never made sense. It's never occurred to me to not say the thing that was on my mind. But after eating lunch with Socks, Jas, and Kisa (Jas's non-cousin BFF), I kind of get it. Most of the stuff they discuss involves people I don't know or events I've missed. Plus, it's hard to get a word in.

Jas and Kisa don't talk as fast as Socks, but their rhythm is hard to break into. I wonder if it's like that with Cady, Kaytee, and me. Every time I feel like I have something to add ("Sure, Ms. Vasquez has great hair for a teacher" or "Two pumps of caramel in my blended iced coffee is too much" or "The new superhero movie was all right, but the action sequences were so green-screened") the conversation skips to the next thing before I'm able to insert an opinion. Jas no longer seems mad at Socks about the shoe thing earlier; they're zipping back and forth about some annoying family barbecue coming up. I'm not sure if I'm included in that forgiveness. I'm about to apologize for my blunder when a girl with long brown hair and a not-subtle headband saunters up to our table.

"Sup?" she says, looking at nobody in particular.

"Hey, Lilly, this is KT," Socks says.

"Oh. Hi. Um, are you new?" Lilly's lips are very shiny, like she's spent lunch applying gloss instead of eating.

"Yep," I say. "Hot outta Iowa City!" I gear up to answer some questions about cornfields, cows, winter, or any other Iowa stereotypes, which I'm really happy to talk about because missing home is all that's been on my mind as I've dolphin-doodled.

"Chill. Okay. Well. I just came over to remind y'all that the party part of my bat mitzvah this weekend will have a DJ. Also known as my older brother's girlfriend. Hashtag she's awesome. She has her septum pierced, but, like, for real," she informs us, and I can't help but bring my hand to my nose. "Anyway, y'all have to make sure to dance a lot, okay?"

"Ayden's coming, right?' Jas asks, looking around to make sure he's not within earshot.

"Def. Everyone is coming." Lilly stands there for a second. She fidgets with the notebook in her hands. "I'm sorry that you're not invited, KT. It's just that the invitations went out over the summer before I knew you, and my parents are, like, really strict about not going over budget. So, I can't . . . you know."

"It's okay," I squeak, wanting this awkward half apology to end. I hate watching other people feel uncomfortable. It's like nails on a chalkboard. "It's hashtag chill."

"Cool." Lilly flips her hair. "Extremely accurate dolphin, by the way." She points at my napkin doodle. "Are you sure you're from Iowa?" She laughs at her own joke but doesn't wait for me to answer. "Gotta run. My fries are getting cold. Ugh. Cafeteria fries. Can't wait till high school when we can go off campus for real food. Later!"

I don't necessarily want to go to Lilly's bat mitzvah. I wouldn't know anyone there anyway. I don't even totally know what happens at bat mitzvahs, except that there's dancing, apparently. But I do know, now, that it sure sucks not to be invited. That just would never happen back in Iowa City.

Iowa City. It's eleven a.m. here, so ten a.m. in Iowa. Cady and Kaytee are still in class. Part of me wants to tell Socks or Kisa or even Jas that the secret to making fries delicious, at least in IC, is mixing mayo and ketchup together for a dip, and that my BFF Kaytee always brought her own baggie of Old Bay Seasoning from home on French fry days. But they're so caught up in conversation about what they're wearing to Lilly's bat mitzvah that French fries are way too off topic at this point.

I think back to my second-grade teacher and the balloon breaths. I take some. I still feel the same. Aka bored and sad that I'm not in IC, where I would certainly be less bored and not sad. My mind wanders to Cola and the training note: *5–6 deep breaths in the AM or PM.* I wonder if that's what he's up to right now, late in the morning. If so, I hope the breathing helps him more than it did me.

I've scribbled two more dolphins by the time lunch comes to an end. One could be Sammy, and one is a little bigger, so I guess that's her mom, Luna. And the last, without a doubt, is a portrait of Cola.

After school, I wait at the corner curb for Dad to pick me up. **Three minutes**, his last text said. Dad is extremely accurate when running late. I'm still defrosting from a day in front of the AC, so I don't mind waiting. The muggy afternoon air feels great.

Socks darted off after our last class because she's signed up for the after-school program. "An abomination of picked-over art supplies, nonsense, and chaos," as she described it. Yikes.

I take out my phone to text Dad and clarify that I'm on the far corner by the tallest palm tree (the corner closer to the school's entrance doesn't have a sidewalk ramp, which is annoying). I get distracted by a trio of girls leaving campus together, headed my way. They're laughing and they still look shiny in their back-to-school outfits. One of them pulls out her phone and shrieks, "OMG we need a Day One photo!" She sees me, and I do my best to pretend I wasn't staring at them. A for effort, C for effect, I'd say.

I miss Cady and Kaytee. I try another balloon breath. It's been a long day of smiling and introducing and observing and not knowing. I feel tears rush to my eyes. I blink fast so they'll evaporate before the unfortunate event of an overflow.

"Hey!" a voice calls. It's the shrieker. "Would you maybe be able to take our picture?"

I blink away the last of the extra eye moisture and plaster a sunny Florida smile on my face. "Of course."

She jogs over to me and hands me her phone.

I snap half a dozen photos. The three girls slightly change their pose every time. I don't know them. In fact, I've never seen them before, but I find myself wishing they'd invite me into their picture. Weird, I know.

* * *

Later that evening at dinner—an extravagant meal of delivery pizza—Dad and Lucy ask how my day was. I say it was fine. Because it was. It was fine. No first day of school meltdown disasters. No bullies, fights, or fallen tears. I don't offer to elaborate, though. My head has a lot to work out and I'm not ready to put it all into words.

Fine isn't great, fine isn't fantastic, fine isn't exciting. Fine isn't really even that good.

Being the new kid just . . . doesn't feel all that different from swimming in an oversized life jacket. *Doable, technically not life-threatening, but doesn't feel quite right, either,* I think as I munch on a burnt crust.

A part of me wonders if Cola felt the same after his first day at Dolphina Cove. Stray fish and swarming seventh graders, seaweed and teal lockers, murky water and confusing hallway layouts. Same energy, when you think about it. Maybe he misses the open ocean and his old dolphin friends like I miss cornfields and Katies.

I feel you, Cola.

That night, Lucy comes into my room as I'm getting into bed. I'm still not used to this whole separate-room setup.

"Tell me more," she demands.

"Well . . ." I begin, "I spent most of my day with someone named Socks who compares her social appetite to an avocado."

Lucy laughs. "Is that a good thing?"

I think about it for a moment. "Yes, actually. How was your day? Is the high school super teal, too?"

Lucy laughs again. "Very teal."

"Did you make friends?"

"Not sure."

"Same," I say. "Was everything different and weird and like being in a fun house with wonky mirrors that distort everything?"

"Maybe. That sounds right."

"Do you wish we were back in Iowa City?" That's what I've been meaning to say all along, I realize. That's the Sister Secret I'm waiting for.

"No. No, I don't." Lucy gives my hair a tug. "Sweet dreams, KT Lady."

As she's about to shut the door behind her, I say, "You have to leave it open! For the ghosts to escape."

"Oh, right," she replies. "My bad."

How could Lucy forget?

"It's okay. Sweet dreams," I whisper to Lucy's back as she turns to go.

Something about my voice reminds me of Socks and the way she sounded on our first ride in the teal elevator.

I want to ask Lucy a question, but I'm afraid of what the answer might be.

Chapter 9

The next few days of school, I get lost twice and am late for class when the elevator takes too long. I wear an outfit I deeply regret on Wednesday, not because anyone says anything about it, but because I completely underestimated the fact that pit stains are still possible in tundra temperatures. I discover the bathroom on the first floor doesn't have trustworthy locks. I'm blinded by teal.

I'm sure there will be more surprises to come.

The main differences between Iowa City and Fernbank are obvious. The hallways being outside thing. The teal everywhere thing. The fact that I know nobody and nobody knows me thing. But as the days go on, more differences come out.

Some kids have Southern accents, some don't. That's new.

A lot of girls here wear flip-flops. After school, when the dress code doesn't matter, the dudes who think they're cool put on saggy beanies even though the temperature is in the eighties. Both boys and girls tend to wear oversized sweat-shirts. A lot of boys don't seem to wash their faces much. On second thought, that's probably a middle-school-boy thing everywhere.

I think people laugh more in Iowa City. Not that kids don't seem happy enough here. I just remember there was more laughing back home.

I keep imagining Fernbank Middle but with the familiar faces from Iowa. That would make the teal so much less . . . teal.

Socks doesn't ditch me after the first day, which I appreciate, and she continues to talk and talk and talk. She's nothing like Cady or Kaytee; she's definitely more hyper than my friends back in IC. We don't have inside jokes yet, and she sometimes laughs at things I don't think are funny. I'm not sure I'd ever have a joint birthday party with her, but I appreciate the company. I continue to sit at her lunch table.

At the end of the day, there are so many differences between Fernbank and IC that it's impossible to keep track of them all. Still, I can't help but try. Comparing the two feels as natural as my instinct to put sprinkles on a scoop of ice cream.

Then, on the third day of school, a flyer taped to the (teal) wall catches my eye:

Fernbank Constitution *Needs YOUR Talent!*

Are YOU an opinionated person who wants their views heard?

Do YOU want to see your writing in print?

Do YOU have what it takes to be a journalist?

When: Thursdays, 2:45–3:45 p.m.

Where: Room 207

First meeting tomorrow!

Yes, yes, and yes! Iowa City Middle doesn't have a school paper. Finally, one comparison that doesn't totally stink.

Plus one, Florida.

I ask Socks, Jas, and Kisa about it at lunch. I'm not sure if I'm permanently invited to sit at their table, so I'm glad I have a question (aka a purpose) as I approach. They're all already seated when I pull up, so I'm stuck at the tundra side. Luckily, after the first day of school, I don't leave the house without a backup garment. I twist to unzip my backpack, which hangs on the back corner of Sprinkle, and pull out my hoodie. Nobody objects to my presence, so I take a deep breath and spit it out.

"What's the deal with the *Fernbank Constitution*? I want to sign up. Is that like a totally not chill thing to do, though?" Not that it would deter me from signing up. I don't think. I just want to know what I'm getting into here. Reduce the probability of surprises.

“I’m all about activities,” Socks says. “Very helpful for college.”

“I didn’t know we even had a school newspaper,” Jas says as she chips lavender nail polish off her pinkie.

“Hashtag ambitious,” Kisa adds.

Hashtag I can’t wait.

* * *

Room 207 is a real haul from my last class of the day. When I arrive on Thursday afternoon at two fifty, a very tall and very skinny eighth grader (whom Socks had pointed out earlier—“He farted in the middle of our state math test last year but denied it was him even though it was *so* obvious to everyone it was”) in a green bow tie paces as he speaks to a room of about ten.

“I know this is the first meeting, but I’m not interested in anything short of excellence. I’m accepting pitches as of this moment.”

I nestle Sprinkle into a space in the back of the room. Nobody seems to pay my late entry much mind. Phew.

A boy with damp-looking hair is first up. “I envision a think piece called ‘The Simple but Hard Things in Life.’” He leans back in his chair with his arms crossed as he speaks. Overconfidence is never attractive.

“Go on,” Green Bow Tie commands.

“Just throwing ideas out there off the top of my head, but

think: picking up a slice of pizza without ripping off the cheese, eating ice cream without getting it on your mustache . . ."

Next to me, ever so quietly, I hear a muffled, "You wish." I follow the sound of the whisper to find a boy slumped in his seat. He wears black canvas sneakers, black socks, black pants, and a Hawaiian shirt. An old-fashioned camera rests in his lap.

He looks fun. Mischievous and fun. And cute. If you care about that sort of thing.

Our eyes meet and I shoot him a smile. My smile is returned with a grin, and then a goofy face that involves him slightly crossing his eyes and sticking out his tongue. Without thinking, I pretend to catch a bubble in my mouth and bat my eyelashes. He cracks up, and I stifle a laugh.

Green Bow Tie, aka Miles, continues with pitches. Other hare-brained ideas are met with moderate enthusiasm. Hawaiian Shirt Camera Boy, Juan Carlos, promises a photo essay on something mundane yet profound and "dexterous." That gives me an idea.

I raise my hand.

"Yes, in the back? You're new?"

I've been asked that question like a gazillion times already this week. Duh, if you don't know me, I'm probably new. I grin anyway.

"Hi. Yes, I'm KT. What about a 'Day in the Life Of' column?"

I suggest. The moment the words are out, I start to get excited.

"Tell me more," Miles encourages.

"Like a little slice of life from someone or somewhere you wouldn't necessarily think about. Just to offer an experience of what it's like to live in someone else's shoes."

"Intriguing." Miles rubs an invisible goatee with his index finger and thumb.

"It could be an ongoing column with a new subject in every edition," I explain. "I can interview people near and far to get all kinds of interesting insights."

"I like it, newbie," Miles says. "Run it."

I feel a wave of excitement. My cheeks blush. I sense Juan Carlos glance in my direction, but I keep my eyes trained forward.

Miles tells us all pieces for the first edition are due on October fourth. Yes, the same October fourth that is my thirteenth birthday. I decide that coincidence must be good luck.

The first *Fernbank Constitution* meeting comes to an end (a full seven minutes overtime) and the room disperses. I text Dad to let him know I'm on my way out. I see through the windows that it's about to pour any minute. The sky is dark, like a bruise. Dad better be outside. I'm not trying to get caught in the rain. Iowa has tornados, but according to Socks, Florida has monster storms this time of year. Looks like she wasn't exaggerating.

As I'm about to put my phone away and get going, Juan Carlos walks by and says, "Chill idea, new KT."

My stomach flutters.

I leave the first newspaper meeting with a tingle of Florida-sized excitement. Now all I have to do is come up with my first subject.

Chapter 10

"I'm going to the mall to meet up with a few girls from school," Lucy tells me Saturday afternoon. "You want to come?"

It's nice of Lucy to invite me. I rarely turn down an opportunity to hang out with her friends. And the mall is a particularly great place to kick it because the floors are flat and glossy, glossy, glossy (Sprinkle's dream terrain). But . . .

"I have a video chat date with Cady and Kaytee," I say. "Thanks, though!"

"You sure?"

I think about it, but I don't want to ditch my friends. It's been a long week. "Yeah. Next time!"

I'm pretty sure Lucy rolls her eyes at me as she walks out the door.

Teenagers.

"Love ya," she calls right before the screen door slams.

"Love ya back," I reply.

I'm planning on catching up on this week's most-read articles from the *New York Times* when Mom and Dad call me into the living room. They're sprawled out on the couch, but push themselves up to seated position when I arrive. The couch is too small for our new house, but I'm glad they brought it anyway. Lots of memories on that guy. A muted college football game is playing on the TV.

"Your dad got a new gig," Mom informs me. That's what they always call his electrician jobs.

"That's cool, I guess. Where?"

Mom and Dad look at each other before answering.

"Dolphina Cove," Dad says finally. "Apparently your mom and that sunburned lady at the front desk—"

"Annie," Mom and I say at the same time.

"Right. Annie. Well, your sweet momma and her got to talking, and Mom spilled the beans that I'm an electrical wizard."

Mom rolls her eyes and gives him a playful swat. They're in love. They've been a couple since college and they're still, as Mr. Jake always commented, "sweet on each other."

They go on to explain that Dolphina hired Dad to fix the panel for their backup generator. Since it's hurricane season, they don't want to take any chances by waiting until it's in further disrepair. Because he works during the day, and they'd rather go to him directly than through a company, they've arranged for him to come after his other job.

"So you have a choice," Mom says. "On the days when Dad

goes to Dolphina, you can go to the after-school program at Fernbank. I spoke with Principal Lim and they have a really exciting art and creative writing program."

I remember how Socks described it. An "abomination" of sorts. No, thank you.

"Or just meet Lucy here after school?" I ask.

We used to do that back in Iowa City. Usually Mom or Dad was home after school, but last year there was a phase where Dad worked late and Mom couldn't get home until five. Lucy and I had two hours of parent-free sister time. That's actually when our Sister Secrets started.

"That works for me." I'd have to take the bus, which comes with its own challenges, but the after-school program sounds way worse.

"Well," Mom starts, "Lucy is playing volleyball and has some computer programming club thing. I'm not sure when it starts, but I want to let her have some freedom."

I work really hard not to roll my eyes. Okay. *Freedom.* Whatever that means. Like hanging out with me is prison.

"Okay, so what's the other option?" I ask again.

Dad says, "You can come with me to Dolphina Cove. Annie says it's cool if you want to do your homework in the office or on a picnic table if it's nice outside. It'll just be a few afternoons for a week or two. Temporary."

My mom adds, "There's been a lot of change recently for you girls, and we want to be sensitive to that."

"Then we probably should have stayed in Iowa." I regret it the second the words come out of my mouth. That was dumb. And mean. I see my comment land on my parents' faces like tiny razor cuts. "Sorry."

Mom reaches forward and pats my hand. "It's okay. I know this has been hard." Mom has ninja forgiveness skills. Or, to put it in psychology professor terms, empathy.

I take a balloon breath. It doesn't calm me down, but it does give me another moment to think.

I remember nights in IC when Mom and Dad thought I was asleep and I heard them whispering about bills and getting approved for more credit cards. I also remember how mopey Dad was between gigs. He's the type who needs to stay busy. We both are. It's good that Dad has the extra work.

Plus, the after-school program sounds like just another version of actual school—another scenario to adjust to.

Dolphina Cove, on the other hand, is familiar. Tara, Jolie, Natalia, and even Annie will be there. Those picnic benches are the most scenic place ever to do math homework. I'll roll Sprinkle carefully over the gravel in the parking lot and wind up early to get over the sidewalk canyon on the path to the dock. I can watch Cola splash around from a safe distance. Most important, I don't have to get in—or even go within falling-in-the-water-accidentally range of—the lagoon. At the end of the day, I still love dolphins.

The choice is obvious.

"Let's Dolphina Cove it up," I say, raising my hand for a high five. Dad's palm meets mine for a crisp slap.

"Are you sure?" Mom asks.

"Don't worry, Mom. You're not putting me back in the scene of a trauma, and I won't be at all triggered." Sometimes it's best to speak her psychology language to get through to her.

Though I will admit that the idea of getting in that lagoon again gives me goose bumps all down my neck.

Chapter 11

On my first afternoon at Dolphina Cove, I park Sprinkle at the end of the picnic bench closest to the lagoon. Annie offered to escort me down, but I told her I had the situation under control. Dad's somewhere behind the trainers' office checking out whatever he's been hired to fix. No one's in session and no dolphins are in sight. It's one of those days where the sky is thick with clouds, but it's muggy as ever. The hair at the base of my ponytail is damp with sweat.

"She's back!" I hear Tara exclaim from behind me. I turn to see her walking toward the lagoon, small rubber basketball tucked under one arm, tin bucket overflowing with ice and frozen fish in the other.

"Miss me?" I joke.

"You bet." Tara comes over to give me a hug. "Annie tells me your dad is the genius who's going to fix our backup generator."

I nod. "Are you training Sammy again today?"

"Not right now. Cola and I are going to do some bonding,"

she explains, and I realize that's what I was hoping she'd say. "Nothing crazy. He's still getting used to it here, and we're still getting used to each other. I wrote a behavior chain last night that I'm excited to try out."

I nod like I understand everything. Then realize I don't, so I ask, "What's a behavior chain?"

"Oh, a behavior chain is essentially just written steps to teach a dolphin a new behavior. Today we're working on station training—getting him to face me when I bridge—and target training. Eventually, once he has that down, I'll use the target to teach him how to leap!"

"I think he might know that already," I say, remembering when he was showing off the other day.

Tara laughs. "True. But I want him to associate it with the bridge, so the move isn't only at random. Anyway, I'm excited. I love me some Cola."

Tara walks down the path toward the dock. Without other guests, Dolphina feels quiet and private, just like the morning of my first visit. Jolie and a trainer I didn't meet the other day are on fish-cleaning duty, and they wave from the area outside the trainers' office, where they're soaping down and hosing off buckets and hydration tubes. From a distance, I watch Tara begin her session. She sits cross-legged on the edge of the dock and then slowly dangles her feet in the water, moving them back and forth.

Cola arrives, and she plays with him like this for a minute, bridging and feeding him a fish every time he bobs to the surface.

Oh, yeah, this is much better than after-school.

I take out my math homework, but it's hard to focus. I can't understand every word, but I hear Tara talking to Cola and can see his head when he surfaces by the dock. I wish I were closer. Not too close; dangling a limb over the edge of the dock is just a slip or push away from floating in the water. But observing from afar is where it's at. Truly, dolphins are so much more interesting than basically any subject in middle school.

Math, science, and history prove hopeless, so I open my notebook to a blank page to begin brainstorming ideas for my "Day in the Life Of" article.

When I pitched the column, my immediate idea was to write about an aspect of Iowa City life. Obvious choice (or, on brand, as I like to think of it), but still effective. A situation in which I'm an expert, and probably somewhere Fernbank kids know little to nothing about. I make a list of potential days and aspects of life to consider:

1. Winter. First snowstorm. Being snowed in. Snow day!
2. Growing up on a college campus.
3. Tornado drills.

I put down my pencil. Very weather-heavy. I glance down at the lagoon. The mid-afternoon light approaches golden hour.

Other than Tara's voice, the occasional bridge, and Cola's splashing, the air is thick and quiet. Calm.

I pull out my phone and try to video chat Cady. No answer. I try Kaytee. Same. I imagine all the places they could be. In Iowa City, the air is probably starting to get ever so slightly crisp. This time in the afternoon, there's usually a long line outside Jake's Freeze. The gallery wall is full of drawings. College students mingle in the outdoor mall.

Tara's bridge breaks me out of my daydream.

"Cola, you are so cute, I love you so much!" she exclaims. I crane my neck to see what Cola is up to. It seems he's swimming in circles around the lagoon, occasionally charging up to the surface. "Cola, you just have all the energy in the world, don't you?"

I watch Tara hold out the basketball and wait for her bridge, but after what feels like a while, she slaps the surface of the water instead. The sound it makes surprises me like a finger prick. Finally, Cola arrives before her at the dock.

"You are so handsome! Very good, sweet Cola." Tara throws him a fish. He doesn't gobble it up right away. She reaches out to give him a rub on the back, and Cola smiles. Or at least I think he smiles. I mean, dolphins always smile. A moment later, before Tara seems to be done with her rub, Cola submerges himself underwater, concealed once again within the cold, murky lagoon.

Twenty minutes later, Tara's session is over. She returns with the basketball and an empty pail. Her leggings and T-shirt are soaking wet.

"How did it go?" I ask.

Still cheery, but clearly more exhausted than she was just forty-five minutes ago when the session began, Tara says, "We're getting there. Cola's still stuck on a lot of his old habits." She sets the bucket on the ground and stretches an arm overhead.

"Like what?"

"Hunting for fish. I get the impression he was Mr. Popular in his old pod. He's feeling out the new social scene. I think that's why he jumps so much. Dolphins sometimes do that to check out their surroundings. I guess he isn't quite used to it here yet. Luna typically runs the show, so they're working it out. Push and pull," she explains. "I'm going to try adjusting his reinforcement, not always starting with fish. He's still catching a lot of his own in the lagoon anyway. They need to expect the unexpected, I have to remember." She pauses. "Sorry, this is probably more than you ever wanted to know. I'm just running my mouth over here."

I think of Socks. After a few days with her, my standard of what qualifies as "running your mouth" is much higher. "No way. I love hearing all this secret dolphin info!" I exclaim, maybe a little too excitedly. Suddenly, the memory of floating in the lagoon, waiting for Sammy to appear from the depths below, the bridging, the crowd of guests gathered on the dock, the chill of the water hits me . . . Despite the humidity, I shiver. Then, to myself as much as Tara, I say, "I love dolphins so much. I really do."

Tara smiles and sets down her pail. She glances over her shoulder at the lagoon. The dolphins are quiet beneath the surface of the water. When she turns to me again, her face is soft. "It wasn't until I'd already started my first internship at a dolphin sanctuary in Texas that I realized it's possible to both fear and love something at the same time."

I gulp. "Are you sure?"

"Positive. Little-known fact: Fear isn't always a bad thing. It can be a sign of respect."

I think about that for a moment.

"Cola's probably a little afraid right now, too. A lot has changed for him recently," Tara adds.

"Makes sense," I whisper. We're silent for a moment, both gazing at the lagoon. The late-afternoon sun speckles the surface of the calm water. "Were you afraid that you'd always be afraid? When you were in Texas, I mean. Does that make sense?"

"Makes total sense. Maybe a little, yes. But I think that's what also helped encourage me to learn."

I nod.

Tara smiles and picks up her pail. "Anyway, Cola's a sweetie. Sometimes it just takes a while to get used to new surroundings and that's that. Can't rush it. Nothing for sweet Cola to be ashamed of."

I take yet another balloon breath because what Tara said hits a little too close to home. Maybe Cola and I have more in common than I thought.

Chapter 12

Lucy stomps into my bedroom without any actual greeting and declares, "You're coming with me."

"Sister Secret?" I ask, putting down the article on sea spiders I was reading.

"Nope. But it's Friday night and it's time to be in public. We're going to La Bello's."

Fifteen minutes later, we've said goodbye to Mom and Dad, promised to wear our seat belts, and are out the door.

This is an interesting turn of events. Back in Iowa City, I was usually the one with plans Friday nights. Maybe that's because on Fridays I always went to Jake's with Cady and Kaytee and then we slept over at one of our houses. As they say, consistency is key. Lucy spent a lot of the weekend at home playing online video games against people in different states, or sometimes going to whatever college game was in season if Mom or Dad convinced her. Which was rare.

"What's the deal with La Bello's?" The place sounds

familiar. I think I remember Jas mentioning it in relation to Ayden the other day at lunch, but I was only half listening. Jas tells a lot of stories about Ayden or sixth grade that are anti-climactic or repetitive.

"Just meeting some girls from volleyball there to talk shop."

"Shop, huh?"

"You hush," Lucy teases.

La Bello's is in a strip mall. Before she successfully whisked me away, I didn't think to ask Lucy any more info about the spot. I assumed ice cream or gelato. Wishful thinking. As we approach, I see small print under the main sign that reads "Confectioners of Caffeine." Who on earth needs coffee at seven p.m.?

I called ahead to make sure there are no ambush stairs I'd have to worry about. As it turns out, there are two leading to the front door. The woman I spoke to on the phone promised they had a portable ramp they could assist with for the front door. Or we could park in the spillover lot behind the building and use the back entrance.

Back entrance it is.

Once we enter the café, I get it. It's not about the coffee. Well, not *all* about the coffee. There is a serious vibe going on. It might as well be a school dance. I'm surprised there's not a DJ and a disco ball. The place is jam-packed, mostly with kids. Some younger than me and some older. Definitely some my age who I don't recognize. They must be from one of the private schools or something.

"This is . . ."

"Intense," Lucy finishes my sentence. She waves at some girls crowded around a small table across the café.

I follow Lucy toward her friends, and that's when I see them. More like run into them. They take up a long table smack in the middle of the café: Socks. Jas. Kisa. Ayden. EJ. Lilly. Two girls I don't know. And, as an extra surprise, Juan Carlos!

My stomach clenches. Is it too late to turn around and pretend I was never here? They haven't seen me yet.

Oh . . . never mind.

"OMG, KT!" Socks exclaims. "Hi!"

I wave. Lucy turns around, quickly putting two and two together. She slows, so I slow. There's no avoiding it. Socks, and now the rest of the table, have seen me, so I can't turn around. And I can't blink three times and vanish in a puff of smoke (the ideal option). And we have to pass them to get to Lucy's friends, so I can't just wave and keep my distance.

This is the perfect storm. The perfect Friday night Florida thunderstorm.

"You're here!" Socks babbles.

"Yeah, just coming to hang with my sister and her friends." I gesture toward Lucy.

"I was totally going to text you that we were hanging out, but I realized I didn't get your number yet, but I was going to! Come sit with us!" Socks invites me, quickly shuffling her chair to make room between her and Kisa. I don't think Juan Carlos sees me yet. In fact, I'm sure of it. Unless he has eyes in the back of his head. He looks at something on his lap. I blush at the sight of his floppy hair anyway.

"Okay." I'm not sure if I want to, but I also don't *not* want to.

Lucy looks back at me as if to ask, "You good?"

I nod.

"Join us if things get weird," she whispers. "Or text. That works, too."

Lucy knows me so well.

"Hey, everyone," I greet them, almost loud enough for the whole table to hear. Jas says "Hi," but only once Ayden gives me a "Sup?" I've never really talked to him or EJ before, but they've dropped by our table at lunch a few times, so I get their vibe. I don't take their lack of enthusiasm personally.

I pull into the space Socks has made for me. The table's not an ideal height—Sprinkle's arms don't quite fit underneath—so there's an awkward gap between my lap and the table. Lilly and the two mystery girls sit across from me, and Juan Carlos is all the way at the end.

It's a squad, for sure.

Conversation around me resumes and a waitress appears.

"Can I get you anything, honey?" she asks.

I haven't had time to look at a menu. I don't even see a menu. I'm the worst at ordering. Cady and Kaytee hate going to eat with me because I can never make decisions, even at the cafeteria. I quickly survey the table. Everyone else has these extreme-looking concoctions before them, except for Juan Carlos, who stirs a tiny espresso cup with an equally tiny spoon. I have a feeling that if I don't order now, I won't get another chance. It won't be a good look to sit here without a drink.

The waitress is getting impatient.

"Um, I'll have whatever she has," I mumble, pointing at Socks's cathedral of a beverage. "What exactly is that?" I ask Socks after the waitress has left.

"Oh, it's the best. An angel food mocha frappé with an extra pump and a half of caramel. It's their specialty. Well, the extra caramel is my specialty. Socks specialty!" she cheers.

My stomach churns thinking about all the sugar.

"So, you guys, get this," Lilly announces to the entire table, breaking up the mini-flirtation between Jas and Ayden. Jas does not look pleased. "I think Morgan was totally faking it when she said she lost her shoes. My brother's girlfriend says she *saw* her put them behind the DJ booth."

"D-R-A-M-A!" Kisa mumbles, eyes still buried in her phone.

"It's, like, too much," Lilly continues.

It doesn't take me long to figure out she's talking about events from her bat mitzvah. I listen and make sure to laugh and nod when everyone else laughs and nods, but I can't think of anything to add. My eyes ping-pong around the table in an attempt to keep up with whoever speaks. I play with the end of my ponytail, twisting the tip into a thin rope. My drink arrives, finally. I'm glad to have something to focus on. Before I know it my glass is half empty.

"What are bat mitzvahs like in— Where are you from, again?" Lilly asks.

"Iowa City," I say, wiping my mouth with a sticky napkin.

"Right. The capital."

Wrong. The capital is Des Moines. I decide not to correct her. I don't want her to forget she's finally included me in the conversation and move on to something else.

"So do people do stupid things at the bat mitzvahs there like fake losing their shoes and *not* dancing with girls until, like, halfway through the first DJ set?" Lilly glares at the boys. Ayden and EJ throw their hands up. Juan Carlos is in another world.

"Um. Not sure. Never been to one in IC. Nobody had one in sixth grade."

"Riiiiight. Of course." Lilly draws out the word. She likes to be in control of the conversation, I notice. "So have you done anything hashtag chill since living in Fernbank?" Lilly asks. I wish that Lilly would ask me more about Iowa City and what kind of parties we did have there. I actually do have a lot to say on that subject. Though, on second thought, if she doesn't want to know, I don't want to share something so precious. "It's, like, so boring here," she complains. She doesn't really mean that. It's obvious.

"Well, I actually went to Dolphina Cove right before school started," I say, loud enough for the whole table to hear. Too loud, really.

"Yo, is that where they keep dolphins in cages?" Ayden asks, then cracks up as if he invented comedy. Jas immediately giggles as well.

"Hashtag animal cruelty," Kisa grunts into her phone.

"Actually, it's not like that at all." By the looks on their faces, I don't think any of the present company expected me to speak up. I wasn't planning on it, but the words slipped out. I can't let anyone talk smack about my pals. My pals being Cola, Sammy, Luna, Ginger, and any dolphin I come to meet in the future. "It's really like a research center slash sanctuary."

"But, like, what do you do there? Watch them do tricks?"

Behaviors, not tricks, I think, but don't say.

"You can learn about how they're trained, or pet them or rub their bellies," I explain.

EJ shouts, "Hey, I heard that dolphin fur—"

"Dolphins don't have fur!" Lilly teases. I never thought correcting a seventh-grade boy's understanding of marine mammals could be flirtatious, but Lilly manages that.

"Whatever, skin, scales. I heard that it's mad rubbery, like a wet suit," EJ says.

"Actually," I butt in, "it feels kind of like a wet suit and a windbreaker and a rubber band had a baby." I notice Juan Carlos crack a smile. I hold my breath in an effort to suppress a blush.

"Hashtag specific," Lilly says.

Should I be embarrassed that I know so much about dolphins?

"I've always wanted to go to Dolphina Cove," Socks admits. She gets quieter when EJ is around. This is the first time I've heard her voice in two hundred seconds, at least. "Did you swim with them?"

My breath catches. I don't want to lie. But I also don't want to tell the truth.

"Wait," Ayden interjects. "Can you swim?"

"OMG, rude!" Socks hisses, but it's too late. The entire conversation has come to a halt, the energy at the table changed. Jas stares at the floor. Kisa's eyes remain on her screen, but

I can see her back tense. Lilly's mouth is frozen mid-smile, her anonymous friends whisper very quietly to each other, and even Juan Carlos appears uncomfortable. He taps a stirrer against his empty espresso cup. They all feel awkward. I can tell. I've witnessed conversations hit a wall like this a gazillion times.

"What? I just wanted to know!" Ayden responds. Then, "Is that a crime?"

Only—and I mean *only*—because Ayden looks directly at me when he asks this do I have the courage to answer.

"So not arrest-worthy." My joke breaks the ice, and I continue, "Yes, I can swim. I swim with my arms. See?" I move my arms like I'm doing breaststroke, then freestyle, then backstroke. I'm about to do butterfly when I decide to drop it and throw up a peace sign.

"See, we're cool, right?" Ayden asks.

"We're cool," I say.

"Chill." Ayden reaches across the table and in for a fist bump. Before we make contact, the front of his hoodie somehow catches the straw of Jas's drink, tipping it over. Saucy, half-melted coffee frappé and whipped cream shoot across the table in my direction.

Socks jumps back, but I don't have enough time to get clear of the danger zone. The cup lands on the ground between us. Upon impact, whipped cream splatters.

"Aww man, not on Sprinkle," I lament. A big hunk of whipped cream has landed on her front wheel, just out of my reach.

"Sprinkles? Where?" Socks asks. I noticed that she'd run out of pocket M&M's a while ago.

"Oh, that's just my chair." Have I really not told Socks that's what she's called? "I'm going to go clean up. Excuse me."

Thus begins the clunky process of reversing Sprinkle away from the giant table. I get caught on Socks's chair for a second before I'm free. Only once my back is turned and I'm en route to the restroom do I hear the conversation resume.

When I return from the bathroom, I don't have much else to occupy myself with. My drink is empty. I check my phone in case Cady or Kaytee texted (they didn't). Lilly whispers with her two friends and Kisa plays on her phone. Jas and Socks bicker, Ayden flicks a sugar packet through a makeshift field goal EJ makes with his hands. Juan Carlos is gone. I'm surrounded by multiple conversations I'm in no way a part of. I hang for a few minutes, not sure where to look, where to listen, or what to do. I check my phone again. Still nothing to look at there. Explaining my aquatic skills to Ayden and company really took it out of me. Or maybe it was something else that wiped me out.

I text Lucy: **Weird.**

A minute later I feel a tug on the back of my ponytail.

"Ready, KT Lady?"

I give my sister a thumbs-up and tap Socks on the shoulder. She's scrounging for the remains of whipped cream in her empty drink while listening to EJ tell a story in his typical monotone that I can't quite hear.

"I have to go," I say.

"Oh no, are you sure?" Socks asks.

"Yeah, my parents need the car," I lie. "This is my sister, Lucy, by the way."

Socks blushes the way Cady and Kaytee would if they were here. "Hi! I'm Socks! It's not a nickname, it's a lifestyle!" Then, back to me, Socks says, "So glad you could hang for a little!" To top it off, she gives me a strange little side hug.

"Yeah. Good times," I say, mustering as much energy in my voice as possible.

Socks starts to turn back to EJ when she says, "Oh! Selfie!"

"Meet you outside," Lucy says.

Socks digs her phone out of her mini backpack and holds it high above us for the optimal angle. I think of the girls on the sidewalk after the first day of school. I desperately wish they were here to witness this moment. Socks makes a silly face, and I smile so big my molars are on full display. "One more, fully crazy!" Instinctively, I catch a bubble in my mouth and flutter my lashes. Socks pretends to pick her nose, which is a very strong choice, in my opinion. We both burst out laughing.

Socks hands me her phone. "Here, type in your number. I'll text it to you."

I bid the rest of the table farewell and I'm out. I'm at the back door, about to begin the slightly tricky maneuver of pushing it forward, when, like magic, it opens. Before me stands Juan Carlos.

"Whoa," I say.

"Yo," he replies.

Behind him, Lucy gently honks Beluga's horn.

Neither one of us moves. He holds the door, I stay in the doorway.

"That's my ride," I say, pointing to the enormous dented minivan.

Juan Carlos looks over his shoulder. "Tight."

"Yeah. Tight," I repeat.

"Well, see ya." Juan Carlos takes a step back so I can pass.

"Have a great night!" Ugh. What a stupid thing to say. I'm not a cashier.

I'm halfway to the car when he calls, "Yo, KT." I turn my head. His floppy hair is just the floppiest in the early evening light. "Lilly's bat mitzvah wasn't that great, FYI." Lucy honks again, a little louder this time. Of all the times for her to be impatient. "See ya at school."

"See ya there!" I belt with the actual enthusiasm of a professional dolphin trainer, then head for Beluga.

As I wheel toward Beluga, Lucy steps out to help with Sprinkle. I get into the front seat and look over my shoulder for another glimpse of Juan Carlos. He stays in the lot taking photographs.

"Spill it," Lucy commands as she pops back into the driver's seat after loading Sprinkle into the back.

I don't know where to begin. In the rearview mirror, I can see that Juan Carlos hasn't gone back inside. He's still standing outside, snapping pictures of something on the ground. I think it's a puddle.

"Well?"

Balloon breath.

I tell Lucy everything that happened. How the people I've been eating lunch with every day of seventh grade all made plans and didn't invite me. How Lilly can't get over her bat mitzvah. How Ayden thought I couldn't swim. I leave out the part about how Juan Carlos's floppy hair makes my stomach flip.

"I'm proud of you for hanging, KT Lady."

"Thanks," I mutter. "This Friday night would be so much better back home. Home being Iowa City," I clarify.

Lucy doesn't speak again until we're stopped at a red light.

"Sister Secret?" she asks, her eyes focused straight ahead.

"Duh, but I don't know if I can handle Tommy's," I say. My

stomach feels crazy after that frozen coffee swirl thing.

"Not Tommy's. Just something I've been thinking about for a while. Fernbank is never going to feel like Iowa City. It's different and it's new. But new isn't always bad. You can't compare coffee and ice cream. They're different things."

I think about what she says for a second before my mind wanders once again to all the fun I'm missing while I'm stuck down here in overcaffeinated Florida.

"Yeah," I say, managing a half smile. "I guess you're right."

* * *

I'm plugging my phone in to charge before bed when a text from Socks appears. It's the selfie from La Bello's. Beneath the photo, the text reads:

Cuuuuuuute. Fun hanging 4 realllzzzz.

I quickly type back the celebration emoji and a balloon emoji. When I lock the screen, a photo of Cady, Kaytee, and me appears. It was from earlier this past summer. We were all tan and laughing hysterically, though now that I think about it, I can't exactly remember why.

Did Socks want the selfie as a way to ask for my number without drawing attention to the fact that she didn't have my number, and that's why she didn't invite me to hang out in the first place? Or worse, did she just take the selfie because she didn't want me to feel left out? Would that be so bad? I *don't* want to be left out. Maybe Socks was really being nice. Maybe she means it.

But maybe not. I don't know her well enough to be certain, I guess.

The truth is, though, I look happy in both pictures.

Chapter 13

I spend the rest of the weekend texting with Cady and Kaytee, lazing with Sprinkle in the driveway while Dad tries to power-wash the outside of the house, and looking up scholarships for youth reporting programs. Oh, and basically obsessing about everything that happened at La Bello's.

I want to believe what Socks said, that she was so glad I was there and she would have invited me if she had my number. I mean, there's really no way she could have gotten it. Nobody at school had it.

I want to believe her. And I mostly do. Still, there's no way around it. Being left out, even if it's accidental, even if it has nothing to do with new classmates liking you or not, is a bummer no number of balloon breaths can easily fix.

When Monday morning comes around, I'm almost excited to have somewhere to go. Hopefully math, at the very least, will distract me. Worst-case scenario, I can invent new ways to generate body heat. It's almost October, and

Fernbank Middle still has that AC on extra high. Brrr.

Socks isn't in homeroom. When Ms. Vasquez takes attendance, one of Lilly's friends from La Bello's announces that Socks is "way sick." I haven't talked to her since she sent me the selfie Friday night, but she has my number now. We have basically every class together except for math. She could have texted me to tell our teachers.

5–6 balloon breaths in the AM or PM.

I take a gigantic inhale and a long exhale. I make it to a slow count of seven before all the air is out of my lungs.

"You sound like wind," Lilly's friend comments as Ms. Vasquez starts in on morning announcements.

I feel like a storm, I think.

When lunchtime comes along, I don't have it in me to even approach Jas and Kisa. Not without Socks. I take a detour to the farthest corner of the cafeteria. En route, I notice Ayden and EJ talking to the girls. Ayden sits in Socks's normal seat, while EJ stands at the end of the table where I usually park Sprinkle. The girls are busy flirting with the boys, and the boys are busy pretending they don't know the girls are flirting with them. Juan Carlos joins them a beat later. He seems to listen to the conversation for a moment before putting on his headphones.

Fernbank Middle is a jigsaw puzzle. I feel like a piece that was accidentally packaged in the wrong box.

All those old teen movies were right. Eating lunch alone sucks. As I nibble on the soggy sandwich I've brought for lunch, I realize that I haven't really talked to anyone else outside of the Socks, Jas, and Kisa squad. Now that I think about it, in the Iowa City version of my life, I really *was* a social avocado, keyword *adaptable*. I spent most my time with Cady and Kaytee, but I chatted with anyone and everyone over the course of a typical school day.

Yet another thing that's changed.

A girl with clear-framed glasses sits down at the end of my table and cracks open a Tupperware of edamame beans.

"Iowa is the second-biggest producer of soybeans in the US," I mumble. Mostly to myself, but in case she's curious.

She appears genuinely confused. "What does that have to do with anything?"

I intend to respond, but the truth is I'm not really sure. I spend the rest of lunch staring at sandwich crumbs and blinking back tears.

Chapter 14

After school on Tuesday I go with Dad again to Dolphina. I post up at the same picnic bench. There are two sessions in progress down at the lagoon: Tara works with Cola, and Natalia plays with Ginger.

It's funny how on my first visit I couldn't tell the dolphins apart. Now it seems pretty obvious. It's not just the differences on the outside, like a nick in the tail or a cross-bite. They really do have personalities. Let's put it this way: Cola's a firework and the rest are birthday candles. Birthday candles are pleasantly festive, and wonderful in their own right. But few things compare to fireworks.

The deadline for my *Fernbank Constitution* article is starting to sneak up on me (I guess so is my birthday, but I try not to think about that). I've decided to go for the simple option. Sometimes simple is best. "A Day in the Life of an Iowa City Middle Schooler."

Lucy's latest Sister Secret words of wisdom tumble through

my brain. Coffee and ice cream. At first, I'd planned to make my article read like a compare and contrast. But nobody likes to be spoon-fed. In other words, comparing coffee and ice cream isn't even necessary. The differences are just so obvious. I'll just describe ice cream in explicit detail. Ice cream being delicious Iowa City.

Dad likes to use metaphors in his poems. Maybe he's rubbing off on me.

I start to make a list of my favorite parts of Iowa City. The farmers' market. The haunted houses on Halloween. The Hawkeye flags proudly displayed on every other porch. Looking out from the top of the landing at Schaeffer Hall. The Iowa River. Jake's Freeze. The vintage store with the wide aisles.

Still, I can't figure out where or how to begin writing.

I look up from my mostly blank notebook page when I hear Tara whoop and clap her hands, followed by an extra-loud splash. Cola's leaping out of the water again. I grab my phone and catch the tail end of his performance. I text the video to Cady and Kaytee.

Cady immediately responds. Your reality is insane.

Kaytee follows it up with an enthusiastic !!!!!!!

Is IC more boring than I think it is? I text back. I'm puzzled as to why my list isn't writing itself into my article.

A few minutes later, Cady responds with a picture. Does this look boring?

I flinch when I look at the photo that follows. No. Not boring at all. Not in the slightest. It seems like they tried to take a picture with a self-timer, but they were a second too late landing their pose. They're a whir of hair, jean jackets, and early fall foliage.

But yeah, more boring without you, Kaytee follows up.

I text them back three yellow hearts.

I stare at my list again. Measly. I close my notebook. So over it. May as well watch Cola's training session instead. As far as homework alternatives go, this one can't be beat.

From my view, Cola still appears rambunctious. I'm not certain of what behaviors they're working on today. Tara bridges a lot and throws him fish after fish. A few minutes later, Tara dives from the dock into the water and continues the training from there. I wonder if it's easier to bond when they're both in the lagoon. I remember from my near swim a couple weeks ago that the lagoon water appeared thick and dense. Was Tara ever afraid of what a semi-trained dolphin would do while she bobbed up and down? Does she, too, sense Cola's movements underwater, but find it terrifying that she can't see where he is?

I doubt it.

I remember what Tara said after the last session, how Cola's stuck on his old habits. Hunting and socializing. I wonder who his new dolphin BFFs are. Maybe he misses his old friends from the ocean.

What a bummer.

I watch the remainder of the session. Dad calls to me from the deck outside the check-in office. He's wrapping up, but I wait at the picnic tables until Tara's on her way back from the dock. I'm curious for a Cola update.

"How are the old habits?" I ask. Tara carries an empty pail in each hand, and has a hydration tube thrown over her shoulder. "Seems like he's still flipping on his own terms." I know Tara is trying to bond with Cola, but a small part of me likes that Cola still insists on his old open-water moves.

"I think we're making great progress. And Cola surprised me today!" Tara beams. "He's a real bubble ring pro."

I like that Tara not only talks to me like I'm a human, but also like I know a thing or two about dolphins, though bubble rings are outside of my dolphin-themed vocabulary.

"Bubble rings?" I inquire.

Tara tells me that bubble rings are exactly what they sound like. A dolphin will release air from their blowhole underwater and then use their rostrum (technical term for nose) or flukes (technical term for tail) or their pectoral fins (think: arms) to whip the air into a circular ring of bubbles. "Dolphins like to play with them until they eventually evaporate. What's really cool is that it's something dolphins do both in the wild and here."

That *is* cool. Hashtag cool, even.

"He's showing you his world," I say in amazement.

"Yeah," Tara says. "Actually, that's a really awesome way to put it. I never quite thought of it that way."

I wish I could tell Cola that I'm ready to listen.

I search for "dolphin bubble rings" on my phone while I wait for Dad to finish up in the office. My stomach growls. I'll try to convince him we should stop at Tommy's for a milkshake on the way home.

He's chatting with Annie about something or other. They're mostly out of earshot, but she's giving him compliments on his work. I can tell. One, because Dad is a kick-butt electrician, and his customers always love him because he can work really fast (he says it's to get the job over with so he can get back to his writing, but still). And two, Dad always tugs at his chin hairs when people say nice things about him. Habits.

When the video finally loads, dozens of clips pop up. I didn't expect bubble rings to actually look like literal circles of bubbles, but they do.

Dolphins are just the best.

Each video shows a dolphin creating a perfect circle of air underwater, shimmery round ropes composed of a gazillion tiny bubbles. The rings spin through the water like shiny tops. Some of the videos take place in man-made pools, some are clearly from the ocean, and I imagine at least some are of dolphins swimming in open-water lagoons like Dolphina Cove's. The water in every picture is a clear, Windex blue.

The dolphins all look like they're having so much fun. I can easily picture Cola making bubble rings now, both here and in his past life, before he arrived at Dolphina Cove.

My phone either freezes or loses service. Maybe both. I take a balloon breath and look out at the lagoon. The water is darker and more impenetrable than ever.

Chapter 15

After nearly five days of the stomach flu, Socks is back in school, and I've regained the courage to sit with her squad at lunch. Socks talks extra fast, like her words will eat her if she doesn't get them out, describing some soupy concoction she made that "fixed her stomach once and for all." She seems a bit more jittery than usual. Maybe she went into sugar withdrawal while she was recovering. While doodling a (surprise, surprise) dolphin on the back of my hand, I notice Jas drawing with a fancy pink pen in her notebook. The margins are filled with designs for dresses, sneakers, and jumpsuits.

"I'd wear any of those," I compliment.

Jas rolls her eyes. "They're not nearly done yet."

"Boom!" Kisa exclaims, dropping her phone on the table and lifting her hands in the air as if she's won a race. She's just beaten her high score at some game that she explains but I don't totally follow. Something to do with surfing and farming.

I'm grateful, I really am, to have girls to hang with. I'm just not sure they're my people. I don't know much about video games, garlic-infused bone broth, or incomplete clothing design.

That afternoon at the *Fernbank Constitution* meeting, after lecturing the group on the value of a committed beat reporter, Miles insists we use the rest of the time to work on our stories. "The production schedule is tight. If you don't meet your deadline, you don't get your story in print." With that, he wipes the lenses of his glasses on his short-sleeve button-up shirt and says he'll be in his office working on copy if anybody needs him.

"His office is literally the hallway in front of his locker," Juan Carlos whispers to me after Miles has left.

"He's sure got a lot of flair, huh?" I say, stifling a laugh. "Very jazzy."

"So not punk rock."

"*So* not. I was thinking more disco meets techno," I add.

"Could use a side of reggae, if you ask me."

"Def. And an appetizer of . . ." Suddenly I can't for the life of me think of another genre of music that has ever existed. And never before have I so wanted to. "Xylophone?" I try.

But Juan Carlos has walked away. Welp, that was nice while it lasted. A moment later he returns with a chair and sits down next to me. I don't have any classes in this room so there's no cutout desk. It's awkward to reach the table in front of me. But less awkward than if I were at a cutout desk with a lower surface. Well, both are awkward.

"How's your article coming along?" he asks.

Immediately, I blush. I wish there were a way to turn off that reaction. "Okay," I say. "Actually, it's a lot harder than I thought. I'm kind of stuck."

"I'd help you if I could, but words aren't my thing. Pictures make more sense to me." He cradles his camera. I can tell it's precious to him. I take a balloon breath. Still not sure if they do anything.

"How about yours?" I ask.

"Getting there. Wanna see?"

"Yes!" I say, maybe a little too excitedly. Juan Carlos pulls his chair closer so we can look at the screen on his camera together.

"I've been really into reflections lately, so that's mostly what I've been taking pictures of."

We scroll through the photos in silence, letting the images speak for themselves. There are some shots of reflections in mirrors and glass, but even more of water. A half-filled dirty pool, a clean pool. A lot of the ocean. Several of puddles. Maybe that's what he was photographing from the curb that night at La Bello's after Lucy and I drove away.

"I kept trying to catch the moment after the wave crashes

onto the sand. For a split second the water smooths out and is really flat, making it super reflective. It's real fast, though, so it's hard to capture," Juan Carlos explains.

Hashtag wow, I think.

The next photo must be from a dock or a boat because the water is dark and deep. Like a midnight mirror. We linger on this one longer than the rest. The water reflects some clouds in the sky and maybe a wisp of his hair. Or a twig.

"That's from my parents' boat," he says. "My dad's obsessed with fishing. This is what I do when he makes me come with him. I took this the weekend before school started."

"What do you think is underneath the water?" I wonder aloud. I imagine Cola making bubble rings.

Juan Carlos blurts out, "Monsters." I gasp, but he smiles. "Joking. I haven't really thought about it, I guess. If I could see through the water, then there wouldn't be a reflection, which would ruin my project. If that makes sense."

"Are you afraid of anything that doesn't make sense to you?" I manage to say.

Juan Carlos thinks for a second. "Clowns?"

"I agree."

"Ha-ha." He pauses again. "I used to be really afraid of clocks when I was a little kid."

"Clocks?"

"The hands reminded me of swords or something. I dunno. I told you, it doesn't make sense. But then I found a busted one in the garage, and seeing all the gears in the interior made me kind of interested in learning how they worked. I got kind of obsessed with figuring out their inner workings or whatever. For a minute I wanted to be a professional clock fixer."

I can't help but giggle. Juan Carlos would be the cutest professional clock fixer ever.

"Anyway," he continues, "once I learned how they worked, I wasn't so afraid anymore. Some of the first photos I took were close-ups of the insides of clocks. Taking pictures helps me take a better look at stuff I might overlook." He stops talking suddenly, and to my astonishment, he blushes. "I'm geeking out."

The truth is, geek looks very good on Juan Carlos.

"It's okay. It's interesting," I assure him. I have to assume I'm blushing now, too.

"Anyway, you're writing a 'Day in the Life' kind of thing, right?"

I sigh. Deadlines are annoying. "That's what I was thinking. I figured the first one would be kind of easy because I'd just do something about Iowa City, where I'm from. But for some reason, it's harder than I expected. Which is weird, because I know Iowa City like the back of my hand and I miss it all the time."

"Tell me about it. What do you miss?" Juan Carlos asks.

So I tell him everything. All the sights, all the smells. I tell him about Cady, Kaytee, and our birthday party tradition, and the epic toga party of three years past. I describe what it feels like to wheel Sprinkle over cobblestones, and how the old houses make my imagination whirl. I talk and talk and talk until everyone around us starts to pack up their belongings. It's already time to go.

I lean forward to get my notebook off the table as Juan Carlos stands.

"Who's that?" he asks, noticing the doodle on the bottom of the open page. It's more like a landscape. A lagoon landscape.

"That's Cola," I share. "And those are the fish he's about to murder."

"Savage."

"Nah, dolphins don't use their teeth to chew food. They swallow their prey whole," I explain. "Yeah, now that I'm saying it out loud, you're right. Savage," I add with a laugh.

"Cute, though."

"The cutest."

Chapter 16

The next week I'm perched at my usual picnic bench at Dolphina, gazing at the lagoon. Since Juan Carlos told me about his photography project, I haven't been able to look at water in the same way. Today it's overcast and windy; the surface of the lagoon isn't as reflective as I'd hoped. Instead, the matte water ripples like wrinkly skin. Still, I bet Juan Carlos could turn it into a rad photograph.

I don't notice Tara approaching until she's just behind me. She carries a clipboard in one hand, a metal pole about six feet long, and a pail overflowing with half-frozen fish in the other. Standard props.

"Do you have a lot of homework?" she asks, gesturing toward the open textbook that I've been ignoring for the past twenty minutes.

I groan. "Um, yes. Big math test tomorrow. I think number stuff is even more boring here than in Iowa City."

"Maybe you just need a break," Tara says, closing my textbook. "C'mon. Follow me."

Tara doesn't need to ask twice. Sprinkle and I jet after her down the path to the docks. We travel and talk.

"Okay, so we're totally not supposed to do this, and I wouldn't risk it if Annie weren't still a little confused about the rules, but I need an assistant today. Would you like to do the honors? Your dad said it was cool," Tara says with a wink.

"Are you serious?"

"Extremely serious. Jolie's dealing with a pet parakeet emergency so Natalia is on double fish-weighing duty. I'm one woman down. I could really use your help."

"Yes, please!" I can't believe she really thinks *I* could help *her.*

"Awesome." Tara wastes no time getting down to business. "Do you remember when I mentioned I'd been working on station and target training with Cola the other day?"

"Of course."

"He's made so much progress, I think we're ready to build on that and start with leaps. So I don't get any of the steps mixed up, it would be great if you could cue me, make sure I don't get off track, and take notes about anything you notice."

"I can definitely do that!"

"You and Cola have such a great connection," Tara adds, and my heart nearly explodes with pride. "I wonder if you might be able to notice something I've missed. He still seems a little out of sorts here at Dolphina."

"I'm on it," I declare in the most professional voice I can muster.

We arrive at the dock, and Tara sets down the fish bucket and the pole and hands me the clipboard under her arm, where the behavior chain is attached. Steps one through twelve are typed in a clear, fourteen-point font.

"I like working with an animal's strengths," Tara explains. "Obviously Cola has a lot of energy, so flipping feels like a natural choice. Since it's an advanced behavior, I also wanted to incorporate a very simple piece of enrichment, or what I refer to in the behavior chain as a *target*."

Ahhh, the pole.

I take a moment to examine the typed behavior chain while Tara settles on the edge of the dock with the pole and the pail. Hearing Tara describe a behavior chain and seeing one written out are two different things. I never realized how much detail and consideration goes into each step, and exactly how much repetition is required. At the top of the page, just below the details listing trainer name (Tara), dolphin name (Cola), and behavior (flip), Tara describes the signal she will use to cue this behavior: *With your right hand, palm facing out, retract the ring finger, pinkie, and thumb so the pointer and middle fingers form a V, like a peace sign.* So specific. I make the signal with my own right hand, testing it out.

"You got it," Tara comments when she sees me doing it.

I drop my hand and feel my cheeks flush. I'm just the assistant, after all, not the actual trainer.

We start with step one: *Station and show the signal.* Tara squats at the edge of the dock (the station) and makes the signal with her right hand. When she's satisfied that Cola's acknowledged the gesture, Tara bridges and throws Cola a couple of fish, which he gobbles up. I make a note that Cola catches them in the air, in case that's important or it relates to his overall athletic ability in some way.

Step two: Tap the target (metal pole) on the surface of the water slightly to the right of the station. When Cola makes contact with the target, bridge.

Step two goes off without a hitch. We're on a roll!

Step three: Repeat steps one and two. When Cola touches the target, loop the target under the surface of the water, drawing a circle. When Cola has followed the target all the way around, bridge once more.

Again, Cola nails step three, no problem.

"Looking good, Cola!" I cheer. "You rock!" I figure more moral support can't hurt.

Step four: Repeat steps one through three. Then raise the target two feet above the surface. When Cola touches his nose to the target, bridge.

The first time Tara tries, Cola overshoots a bit, jumping right over the pole. Since we're practicing leaps, I figure he's just a fast learner, already anticipating what's to come. But Tara insists we repeat step four another three times until Cola gets it exactly right. I record in my notes the outcome of each attempt: (1) jumps over, (2) jumps over, but faster and higher, (3) jumps over before completing the underwater loop. Finally, on attempt number four, Cola follows Tara's instructions perfectly. Satisfied, Tara rewards him with three shimmering fluke, tossing each fish to him one at a time.

"You got it, Cola, great job!" she praises him.

"Go, Cola, go!" I add.

We continue.

Step five: Repeat steps one through four.

I'm noticing a pattern with this behavior chain.

"Tara, this is kind of like a reverse factorial," I inform her with a chuckle.

"A what-a?" she asks as she throws Cola a chunk of ice.

"Oh, just a math thing," I tease.

The session continues for another ten minutes. After step number five, Cola's responses become less consistent. Tara's very patient, but still, Cola seems to have a mind of his own. He has no problem flipping or leaping, that's for sure. But sometimes he does too many or doesn't return to the station when she bridges or signals. Sometimes he just keeps on dancing through the air. Cola flips like Socks talks: nonstop. I think back to something Socks said to me that first day of school: "I talk a lot when I'm nervous." Maybe, like Socks, Cola flips when he's nervous.

I make a note in shorthand at the bottom of the page. *Socks = Cola → nervous talker = nervous flipper.* I'll explain what that means exactly to Tara at the end of the session.

We make it to step number eight before it's time to wrap up. Tara's behavior chain is covered with my handwriting. I'm pleased; nobody would ever accuse KT Wynn of being a poor documentarian. To shake up the session's conclusion, Tara jumps into the water and lets Cola give her a dorsal pull to the middle of the lagoon, where a rogue pool noodle floats. Tara seems completely relaxed as they glide through the water together. When he drops her back off at the dock, noodle in tow, he disappears underwater, only to emerge halfway across the lagoon, launching himself into the air for one of his signature flips.

"You are such a good boy!" Tara squeals, climbing out of the water and onto the dock, feet dangling over the edge. Cola returns dockside and she feeds Cola the last of the fish. "You are the smartest!" Despite the activity of a full session, Cola still appears to have plenty of energy. Hyper, one might say. Another thing he and Socks have in common.

"Do you want to give Cola a belly rub?" Tara asks, snapping

me out of my thoughts. She must see something on my face that I don't realize I'm showing, because she adds, "From the dock. I'll be right next to you."

"O-okay," I whisper.

Tara helps me out of Sprinkle and onto the dock. She instructs me to lie on my belly, parallel to the edge of the water, so my hand can easily reach the surface. As she supports my legs while I use my arms to lower myself down, Cola darts by. Lagoon water slaps against the side of the dock.

Dolphins are just so big. Especially up close.

"Let me know if you want to get up, okay?" Tara offers.

"I'm good," I say. To my surprise, I'm only half lying.

Now that I'm in position, I carefully allow just my fingertips to graze the surface of the water. It's cool. Chillier than I remember. Tara bridges and Cola approaches. I feel my heart jumping in my chest.

"Here he comes," Tara whispers, or maybe she speaks in full voice. I'm not paying much attention to her volume anymore because Cola is five feet away, then four, then three, then an arm's length, and then he's here. I'm about to make contact. I know it's going to be okay—Tara's right here with me—but I see all those Tic Tac teeth, and that giant mouth that swallows fish whole, and I retract my hand as if I've just felt fire. Like a flash of lightning, Cola zips below the surface.

"Let's try again," Tara says gently.

She bridges, and Cola returns. Tara must do another signal with her hand or something, because once Cola's close, he rotates onto his back. His long, pale belly is exposed, like an empty dinner plate or a full moon. He floats in front of me. His eyes are big and his permanent smile looks just as endearing upside down.

"There you go, Cola, good boy," Tara shushes in a tone so soothing it could calm the fussiest baby. "You ready for a belly rub?"

I'm not sure if she's asking me or Cola, but I nod. Tara takes my hand in hers and guides it over Cola's belly. He's so big, and so smooth. I close my eyes and listen with my fingers.

5–6 breaths in the AM or PM.

One . . .

I inhale, keeping my eyes shut. I drift my fingers up Cola's belly toward his pectoral fins. When I open my eyes to exhale, I swear he's looking right at me. Tara lets out a breath with us and leans back. It's just Cola and me.

Two . . .

Inhale. I allow my hand to relax so my whole palm now rests on his stomach. I think I feel his muscles tense, ever so slightly, as if he's deciding if he should swim away. I've reached the top of my inhale so I slowly exhale through my nose. The palm of my hand remains on Cola's pale belly as the air filters out of my body. Cola stays with me.

Three . . .

Inhale. *I know it must be scary to be the new dolphin*, I think, looking right into Cola's eye. I drift my hand over his torso like a lazy windshield wiper. Exhale.

Four . . .

But change can be good. Change can be good, I think on a loop, never once blinking, not daring to break eye contact.

Five . . .

I see you, Cola.

I'm about to inhale on my sixth when suddenly Cola flips over, and with a vigorous splash of his tail, he darts away. I'm almost dizzy with surprise, as if I've just been yanked from hypnosis. I retract my hand and pull it under my chest. Now it feels too risky to let it dangle over the edge.

"You are such a goof, Cola," Tara says after a moment. I notice that she's writing down a note on the very top of the behavior chain in one of the few spaces remaining among the typed instructions and all my handwriting. I wish I could make out her words.

"Y'all really have a connection," Tara says as she assists me back into Sprinkle.

I can only blink and nod. I still feel woozy from our five

breaths. I've never felt so connected to another creature, but it's shocking how that bond can immediately dissolve with one flip of the fin.

As we head back up the path to the trainers' office, I hear clicking sounds coming from the lagoon. I turn just as Cola whooshes out of the water. Rain is brewing in the distance, and with the blustery clouds as a backdrop, Cola is nearly camouflaged as he soars through the air.

"What a stinking show-off!" Tara bellows, shaking her head affectionately.

A major show-off, I think. Emphasis on *show.* Maybe he's just showing. Showing me his world. Cola showing me Cola.

Chapter 17

"Next Tuesday will be my last day of work at Dolphina," Dad casually mentions as he sets down a pot of spaghetti with tomato sauce in the middle of the table. Sunday night dinners are usually one-pot meals. His "specialty." Lucy and I tease that they're more an inevitability because pasta with jar sauce is really the only thing the dude can cook. Mom has a habit of waiting until Sunday to prep for that week's classes, so it's often just Lucy, Dad, and me at the dinner table. I'm fast approaching one-pot overload.

"That was quick," I say. Lucy dishes some noodles into a bowl and places it in front of me. Her headphones are out of her ears and resting on the table, though music still plays like a tired sound track. She's a little sweaty from volleyball practice, but I insisted I was too hungry to wait for her to shower to eat.

"Thanks for being such a trouper. You're an excellent Dolphina wing-girl."

"Hashtag no big deal," I say, dumping a load of Parmesan

into my bowl. The more cheese, the better. "It's been really fun, actually."

"Florida, fun?" Lucy teases. "Never thought that would come out of your mouth."

"Um, rude," I reply, playfully swatting at her arm. "By the way, did you know that dolphins make bubble rings in the ocean and when they live in a lagoon?"

"I didn't," Dad says, before taking an enormous forkful of pasta to his mouth.

"True story. Google it." I go on to tell them about helping Tara work on Cola's last behavior chain, though I leave out the details about the breaths we took together. I'm not ready to release that treasured memory yet. Instead, I conclude, "In lots of ways, dolphins aren't all that different from people. You could probably write a poem about that, Dad."

"Maybe I will," Dad replies. "So what are you thinking for your birthday this year?" Dad asks. I take a bite. Somehow, the pasta is lukewarm. I do my best to not taste it as I chew.

"I don't know," I admit.

"What about that girl who talks a lot? Shorts?" he presses.

"Socks," I mutter.

"You could have her over, and any other people you've met. We'll get out of your hair."

"I don't know," I repeat. "I don't really want to think about it.

Since doing something with Cady and Kaytee is out of the question, I don't care anymore." That's only partially true, but I can't resist the jab.

Dad takes the hint. We finish the meal in near silence. The only sound is the faint notes of a pop song drifting from Lucy's headphones.

Chapter 18

On my final day as the president and founder of the After-School Dolphina Cove Program (official title), Tara immediately invites me to tag along for that afternoon's session.

Hashtag amazing.

First stop is the trainers' office to pick up some fish, where we meet up with Jolie. She juggles two buckets of fish, a basketball, a pool noodle, a hydration tube, and a clipboard. She looks like a cartoon.

"There has got to be a better way," she complains, her clipboard landing on the ground with a smack.

"Why don't you hook a bucket or two onto the handles of my chair?" I suggest. "Her name is Sprinkle, by the way."

"Are you sure?"

"Yeah, Sprinkle's muscles are ripped."

Jolie whispers, "This is so not child labor, if anyone asks," as she hooks a handle onto Sprinkle.

I laugh. "Sprinkle and I are happy to help. Strongest duo Iowa City and Fernbank have to offer."

Jolie gives me a high five, and the three of us head down to the lagoon.

Natalia joins us a few minutes later. She begins her session with Luna, Jolie bridges with Sammy, and Tara perches down on the end of the dock, rubbing Cola's belly. Even though Sprinkle and I are a few feet from the water's edge, I make eye contact with Cola and we take a balloon breath together.

"I think the breathing you did with Cola during your belly rub the other day really helped calm him down," Tara mentions.

"Really?" I ask, though I'm not totally surprised.

"Oh, yeah. I've been trying to get him to breathe with me for weeks, but never combining it with a belly rub like that. You sure have a magic touch with him."

"Thanks!"

"I've been incorporating the belly rub breathing into sessions at different points, and it's made a world of difference."

"I call them balloon breaths," I confide.

"Balloon breaths. I like that," Tara says.

It's fun to watch the three trainers in action up close again, like during my first day. That sure feels like ages ago, the more I think about it. A different world. Now I know so much more about what's going on, like the reason that Tara bridges every time Cola touches a target is because it's part of a carefully planned behavior chain. Or that when Natalia slaps the water, it's not to scold Luna, but to offer her a different auditory cue. Sammy and Luna are no longer attached at the dolphin version of a hip.

As the session goes on, Tara lets me reinforce Cola with fish. He gobbles them up right away.

"That's right, Cola, your BFF is here today," Tara says. I give Cola a wave, and I swear he uses one of his pectoral fins to wave back before shooting out of the water in the most triumphant leap. "You just love to fly, don't you, cutie?" Tara coos.

"Show-off!" I say affectionately. His leaps are still most impressive.

Eventually, Natalia jumps into the water to work on dorsal pulls. I can't help but notice she doesn't wear a life jacket. Hashtag dolphin trainer privileges.

"Sammy, you're having yourself a little dance-off, aren't you!" Natalia exclaims.

"You celebrating, Sammy?" Tara coos. She sits on the edge of the dock, feet dangling in the water. Both Cola and Sammy are away. I think I see Ginger taking a leisurely lap around the perimeter of the lagoon. A lazy afternoon swim. Tara asks, "What's she doing over there, huh?"

"She's making bubble rings!" Natalia exclaims. I'm impressed she can see from where she treads water. It's still so dark, despite the bright overhead sun. "Where'd you learn to do that, cutie?"

Tara and I look at each other knowingly.

"Whoa, I think Ginger and Luna are doing it, too. Bubble ring party!" Natalia wiggles her shoulders and does a mini treading-water dance. "J, throw me that snorkel mask from the bucket."

Jolie tosses it to her. Natalia puts it on and dives below the surface. A moment later she pops up.

"Y'all, this is amazing. I've never seen Sammy, Luna, or Ginger make bubble rings before, especially together!" Natalia cheers. "And now Cola, too!"

"Bubble ring central!" Jolie cheers.

Tara and I watch from the dock. Of course, I can't see what's happening underwater, but their playful energy radiates to the surface and into the air.

"Is that all Cola's influence?" I whisper to Tara.

"I think so." She grins and gives my ponytail a sweet tug. "Like you said, he's showing them his world."

Show-off, indeed.

Natalia pulls off her snorkel mask and starts to swim in. The water around her churns and bubbles, as if she's swimming through a pool of seltzer. "They're having the time of their lives. I wish y'all could see this!"

Me, too, I think. *Maybe I should have swum with them when I had the chance.*

I'm too full of regret to remember to take even one balloon breath.

Chapter 19

When Mom comes home that night, I'm on my bed, leaning against a stack of pillows, notebook open on my lap. Dad's already snoring on the couch. Muted sports highlights flash on the TV. It's late, I should probably be sleeping, too, but I'm determined to make some headway on my article.

After the last-day excitement at Dolphina, it took me a while to wind down. Dad and I stopped by Tommy's for hamburgers and milkshakes. On our way home, I slurped on a chocolate shake while I told him about every last bubble ring detail.

But the afternoon was bittersweet. Saying goodbye to Tara, Jolie, Natalia, Sammy, Luna, and Ginger was tough. I wish I could have given Cola a hug. Or at least another round of balloon breaths. Tara gave me her cell phone number so that whenever I need a pick-me-up, all I have to do is let her know and she'll send me some action shots of Cola, which made me feel a little better. I know that they're just a fifteen-minute drive away—much closer than Cady and Kaytee all the way in Iowa City—but still.

I've had too many goodbyes recently, and I was surprised at just how sad this one made me.

I hear Mom tiptoe down the hallway. She opens the door to my room and peeks in. "You up, KT Lady?"

"Not necessarily," I say, doing my best to get into a convincing sleep position in less than a second.

Mom comes in and sits at the end of my bed. "How was your day?"

I launch into a bubble ring monologue, the speed of which would make Socks proud.

"Wow, that's so cool," she says once I've finished.

"Hashtag incredible," I correct her.

"Hashtag incredible. Could you ever have imagined a few months ago that you'd get to spend so much time with your favorite animal?"

"I guess not." I know Mom is trying to be sweet, but her comment gets me down. "I wish everything in Fernbank felt like Dolphina Cove," I admit. Sometimes it's easier to say what's on my mind if I don't think about it too much first.

"You really feel at home there, don't you?"

"Duh," I mutter. I think about all the cracks in the path from the picnic tables to the docks, and the one big one that requires a wind-up wheel. I remember the way Sammy's fin felt when it grazed against my fingertips just a few weeks ago and the unavoidable scent of fish in the trainers' office. In my mind, I hear Tara teasing Cola for being such a show-off. "Do you think it makes sense to be scared of something but also love it at the same time?"

"Well, if you refer to the DSM-V's definition of attachment theory—"

"OMG, Mom," I interrupt.

"Okay, okay. In non-professor terms, yes. Of course."

I sigh. "I miss Iowa City."

"I know, KT Lady. So do I."

"And I can't even figure out how to write this dumb article that was supposed to be like an ode to my favorite place and myself in a way." I explain my assignment to Mom, who listens without interrupting. "I'm a literal expert on Iowa City. Double expert on being a middle schooler in Iowa City. Why is this so hard?"

Mom runs her fingers through my slightly knotted ponytail. "Maybe that's not the only thing you know a lot about."

We sit together in silence for a minute. I think Mom might be taking balloon breaths, too. I should really put some posters up on the wall, I realize. Or maybe some string lights. I have a photo of Cady, Kaytee, and me on my dresser, and one of Lucy and me when we were little, but that's as far as the decorations go.

Before Mom kisses me good night, she says, "Iowa City is a part of you, KT Lady. It always will be. But it's not the only part."

Chapter 20

"My birthday is next week," Socks tells me during homeroom. Ms. Vasquez has given us the first fifteen minutes to finish any leftover homework. I'm pretty sure she's behind in grading our quizzes from last Thursday.

"Chill," I say. I'm not much in the mood for conversation. We haven't really talked one-on-one since La Bello's. I pretend to check my science homework. I know every answer is right, but I keep my eyes trained on the page. But then because I can't resist, I say, "Libra?"

"Virgo cusp. Venus in Scorpio, but don't go spreading that around."

"Chill," I repeat. I truly have no idea what any of that means.

"You?"

"Libra," I answer. "October fourth."

"Oh wow, so I'm only, like, a couple weeks older than you! It's so not a big deal now in seventh grade, but my other cousin, Jas's sister, says that kind of difference matters when it comes to getting your driver's license."

"Yeah, Lucy says the same," I add.

"Anyway, I wanted to invite you to my birthday party. It's this Saturday." Socks is whispering again so I know she's nervous. Which makes me nervous.

"That sounds fun," I reply without looking up.

Then Socks spits it out. "Look, I still feel really bad about La Bello's. Jas organized the whole thing, and even before you got there, I thought it would have been chill if you knew about it, but I guess I thought about it too late and I didn't have your number. But I felt weird. I still do. Also . . ." Her voice trails off. She's getting to the point now. "We didn't know if you'd be able to get in with Sprinkle, because there are those steps and it can get kind of cramped in there."

"You know that if I avoided all crowded restaurants and places with steps, I'd basically not be able to go anywhere, right?" I snap. I'm getting frustrated, and it's not all Socks's fault. This was never an issue with Cady and Kaytee. We'd just do takeout at LaFonda instead of eating in the café because the stairs there sucked, but if everyone was hanging on the landing of Schaeffer Hall, I'd tell them what I needed, and we'd figure it out. We'd just figure it out. "Sorry."

"It's okay," Socks answers quickly. She blinks back at me

with those big brown eyes. "Actually, I totally don't know what you're thinking."

Awful thoughts creep into my mind, like ants devouring a melted drip of ice cream on a hot summer day.

Isn't it weird that Socks never mentioned her birthday to me earlier?

Balloon breath. Balloon breath. Balloon breath.

Then again, I never told her about mine. Or before La Bello's that Sprinkle is named Sprinkle. I actually can't believe she remembered.

I've never had a hard time expressing my opinion before. But before was before and now is now. I'm not sure how honest I can be.

Balloon breath.

I remember how it felt to talk about Iowa City with Juan Carlos. But mostly how nice it was that he cared to ask. Socks is kind of doing the same thing, I realize.

Balloon breath.

"You know . . ." My voice trails off. "Being new just sucks."

There's more I could add, but that captures it. I laugh because sometimes a smile is the best way through. Socks follows my lead.

"I bet," Socks says. "But I can't imagine what it's like. Everything about my life is here. Fernbank is in my blood, ya know?"

"Fernbank and sucrose," I remind her.

As if on cue, Socks pops a single blue M&M into her mouth. "Honestly, when Principal Lim said we were getting someone new in our grade from out of town, I was really excited. Not a lot changes around here," she admits. I never thought about it that way before. "Change can be good. It's nice to have you spice things up."

"Thanks," I say. Biggest balloon breath of the day. "So . . . your party. What are the deets?"

And just like that, Socks begins a trademark monologue. I smile and enjoy the enthusiasm behind her answer. "OMG, it's going to be so fun. I was thinking about having, like, a big informal thing in the park, and just kind of inviting everybody, but then I thought, 'Socks, you're going to be thirteen. Time to grow up and be picky if you want!' So, it'll be an intimate affair."

"Awesome." I beam, truly thrilled I made the cut.

"So, yeah. You gave me the idea at La Bello's, actually. I didn't know how chill it would be, but then I thought, 'Who cares? It's my birthday, my fun,' and my mom's other first cousin, not Jas's mom, but the other one by marriage, works in the office and got a super discount on tickets so my mom said, 'Fiiiine.'"

"Tickets to what?" I beg. "The suspense is killing me!"

"Oh, sorry. Jas and my mom and her mom always say I'm like the most hyper storyteller. Anyway, drumroll, please . . ."

I tap my hands on Sprinkle's sides for maximum percussive effect.

"Dolphina Cove! We're going to swim with dolphins!"

Chapter 21

The night before Socks's party, Sprinkle and I burst into Lucy's room without knocking. She's sprawled on her bed, playing a video game on her laptop.

"I may not go," I declare. Lucy is slow to look up from the screen. "To the party. To Socks's party. I can back out, right? That's not, like, the rudest thing in the world, is it?"

"What? Why not?" Lucy asks, sitting up. "I thought you and Socks cleared the air."

"We did."

"So what's the problem?"

"I don't think I can do it." My eyes flutter around Lucy's bedroom. I haven't spent a ton of time in here since we moved in, come to think of it. Photos litter the top of her dresser and she's arranged her books according to color in neat stacks, against the wall. I don't know where on earth she got the purple-and-turquoise tapestry hanging over her bed like a mural, but there's a definite vibe going on.

"Do what? You've been to Dolphina Cove more than everyone else in your middle school combined," Lucy says. "That's, like, your territory. You're a dolphin pro."

I roll Sprinkle right up to the edge of her bed. "Okay, can I tell you a Sister Secret? Like the biggest one?"

"Okay . . ."

"When I went to Dolphina for the first time with Mom, I didn't swim with them."

"I know."

"No, I mean, it wasn't because I was sick or nauseous or whatever I said."

"Okay . . ."

"I was scared. Too scared to go through with it." Lucy looks at me with her enormous eyes and takes what has to be a major balloon breath. "Embarrassing, huh?" I whisper.

My big sister reaches forward, past my cheek, and gives my ponytail the most gentle tug. "From everything you've told me, dolphins are beasts. I'm not sure I would have gotten in the water with them, either."

"Well, they're not flesh-eating monsters or anything." I can't let her call my dudes *beasts*. "But, yeah, they're big."

"You should go to the party, KT Lady. It doesn't matter if you swim or not."

"Really?

"Really. Dolphina is your zone. Think of it this way: Iowa flair and Dolphina flair go together like—"

"Rocky road and sprinkles!" I interject.

"Like rocky road and sprinkles," Lucy agrees. "You got this."

What is it about big sisters and their ability to make you feel anything but little?

"Thanks, Lucy." I'm about to leave when I ask, "Hey, can you help me set up my room later? It looks kind of empty and depressing. Like nobody lives there yet."

"You bet," Lucy agrees with a smile. I roll out and am about to shut the door behind me when she says, "Leave it cracked. For the ghosts to escape."

I do as she asks, and we share a smile. One thing that doesn't change across state lines: Tradition is always tradition.

I go to sleep with a full heart.

Chapter 22

I don't think it's ever been hotter at Dolphina Cove. There isn't a single cloud in sight, and the humidity is so high I feel like I'm sitting in a puddle. A puddle of sweat and nerves planted in a palm tree forest.

Dad drops me off fifteen minutes early so I can visit with Tara and the other trainers. Annie, as it turns out, is the relative who got Socks the discount tickets. I'm glad to see her familiar face when I arrive.

"You're a regular," she greets me when I wheel up to the deck outside the check-in office. "Good to see you again, KT." This time, Annie looks me right in the eye.

Annie calls down to the trainers' office to let them all know I'm here, and a minute later Tara trots up to the deck.

"How many bubble rings did Cola make since I last saw him?" I ask after giving Tara a huge hug. She smells like sunscreen and salt water.

"He's gonna be a sculptor when he grows up, I swear,"

Tara says. "Bubble rings are only the beginning."

I giggle. That wouldn't surprise me one bit.

"I've got to go finish getting ready for the session. See you down there!" Tara says.

"Oh, wait— Which dolphins today?" I ask. I feel my stomach flip. Despite all the excitement of seeing everyone again, I can't forget the point of this whole day: the grand finale.

"Sammy and Cola. We gave Cola the morning off so he wouldn't be too zonked for y'all's session. He's been cleared for guest swims for about a week now." Tara somehow answers the question that I didn't quite have the words to ask.

"Hashtag awesome." Just as I had hoped.

I wait on the deck for everyone to arrive. Because I promised Mom, I lather an extra layer of sunblock on my nose and neck. I watch the lagoon. The water is dark, but as I soften my gaze, I allow myself to see the reflection of the blue sky on the surface. As if on cue, a dorsal fin punctures the glassy water. Cola launches into the air for his signature leap.

"Hey, dude," I say.

Socks and Jas arrive first in a gray SUV. In my mind, I name it Manatee. They're already bickering when they step out of the backseat and onto the gravel. Their moms look like taller and more tired versions of their daughters.

The boys all show up a minute later. Ayden smells like

River Mist, which Jas is quick to point out. I give Juan Carlos a wave, but I can't see his eyes behind his sunglasses. He has a smear of white sunblock on his earlobe. I don't point it out. Kisa is last.

"Had to turn around halfway here because I forgot my phone," she offers as an excuse.

"Who is ready to swim with some dolphins?" Natalia asks once we're all gathered. There aren't too many other guests today. A couple from Germany with their seven-year-old twin daughters and a family of five in matching orange T-shirts linger around the deck taking photos. "Follow me down to the picnic table area to get started."

Socks takes the detour with me down the ramp while the other guests descend the stairs.

"So, I did some low-key preliminary research, and did you know that dolphins don't have a sense of smell? And that a pod is like a family of dolphins, which can have as many as one thousand of them?! Hashtag squad goals."

I did know all of that, but I listen to Socks anyway, without interrupting.

Tara leads the information briefing once we have our life jackets on. I ask Jolie for a smaller one than I got last time around. It fits like a glove. Tara gives a brief history of Dolphina Cove and does a speed round of Dolphin Facts 101. She also says that if we're out in the open ocean on a boat and a dolphin pops up, don't feed them.

"Because you're not supposed to feed wild animals, like at the zoo and stuff?" Socks asks. She sits tall in her chair, gobbling up every dolphin-saturated word. "Rawr," Ayden says. EJ and Jas explode with laughter. He's going to need to get a little funnier if he's going to maintain his status as class clown into high school. "Actually," Tara says, "it's because they're going to keep coming back for more once they realize there's an easy food source, and when they bob on the surface of the water for too long, the tops of their heads can get sunburned."

Gosh. As if dolphins could get any more adorable.

"One more thing dolphins and I have in common," Juan Carlos jokes. We share a smile.

I try not to worry about what's to come. Lucy's words echo in my memory. *It doesn't matter if you swim or not.* I hope she's right. Behind Tara, the surface of the lagoon glistens under the relentless sun. Juan Carlos snaps a photo. I hear some splashing, but don't see Cola, Luna, Sammy, or any of the rest of them.

Balloon breath time.

* * *

Here I am again: Sitting on the dock in that Dolphina Cove water chair that isn't Sprinkle. The birthday girl and EJ are set to go first. I'm not sure if she's more excited about swimming with dolphins or standing in a confined platform with EJ.

"Jas, pair with me," Kisa demands, but Jas makes an excuse that she forgot something in her bag, and Kisa should go ahead with Ayden and Juan Carlos. (Odd. Very odd.) When Jas returns a few minutes later I notice her eyes are a little red around the edges.

Jas and I watch in silence as one by one our friends swim with dolphins. Socks shrieks with joy, and even EJ laughs like nobody is watching. I don't think I've ever seen happier human beings.

"Y'all are up!" Tara says after the Kisa group is out of the water. Out of the corner of my eye, I notice Jas fidget with the little key-shaped charm on her gold necklace. My breath is shallow, and the sun toasts the back of my neck. I'm not sure if I am ready yet.

"Why don't you let the twins go first?" I suggest. "I think they're, like, really anxious to get in there. We can hang tight."

I look to Jas, expecting her to challenge my decision, but instead, she just nods. "Yup, totally cool," she says quickly.

Our friends horse around and giggle on the other dock while the blond girls splash around with Sammy and the leader of the orange T-shirt group howls with laughter as Cola leaps over his head.

"Whoa. They're, like, really big," Jas says, as Cola crashes back into the water.

"Hashtag big." Even after spending as much time around dolphins as I have in the past few weeks, that part doesn't get old. Dolphins are just tremendous creatures. No way around it.

"OMG, why do they have so many teeth?" Jas whispers. Her voice is soft in a way I've never heard before. I'm not sure if she's talking to me or herself, but I respond because I know the answer.

"They're not for chomping, if you can believe it. Dolphins don't chew their food. The just use their teeth to snag fish."

"Oh," Jas says quietly. "Okay. That makes sense, I guess."

"Don't worry, they don't bite."

Jas nods.

Soon, the German family and the orange shirts are out of the water. It's just Jas and me waiting to go. Jas's mom has her phone out for pics, and, of course, Juan Carlos has brought his fancier camera. He's been snapping photos since the moment he arrived. I hope I get to see them.

The squad is for sure out of earshot, but Jas whispers again, so quiet I almost can't hear. "Why is that one so thrashy?"

I follow Jas's gaze and land on Cola. I smile. "That's just how Cola plays." We watch him for a moment more. Cola reminds me of a puppy rubbing its back in the grass to scratch an itch.

Suddenly he leaps out of the water. Jas catches her breath. "Show-off," I say with a giggle. "He does that all the time. It's kind of his thing," I explain. Cola lands with a theatrical splash and disappears beneath the surface.

"All aboard, ladies," Natalia calls from the dock. "Good to go?"

I can tell that Jas is too nervous to answer, so I respond for the both of us. "Thumbs-up, Natalia." Then, to Jas, "You'll see when you get closer how happy they are. Plus, their skin feels really cool." Tara pushes my chair a few feet forward onto the mobile dock. Only then does Jas join us.

The dock begins to lower.

Jas's breath catches when her feet touch the water. "Wow. So. Cold."

I can't feel it yet, but I remember. The chill might actually be nice on this hot, hot day.

A moment later the water nears my chest and the dock stops.

"You ready?" Tara asks. I look at the water in front of me. It's dark and it's cold and it's scary, and I have no idea what's under there. But I also know that Cola loves to play, and Tara is an amazing dolphin trainer and not all surprises are bad. "Y'all can swim out to the center of the lagoon together, and then Sammy and Cola will give y'all dorsal pulls back in to where you are now."

I give Tara a thumbs-up and unbuckle from the crazy chair.

I'm about to doggy paddle forward when Jas says, "I'm not the best swimmer."

I see her reflection on the surface of the water before I turn to face her directly. Her eyes dart around the lagoon and she takes very shallow breaths. I balloon breath for the both of us.

"It's okay. That's why you have a life jacket," I remind her. "We can do this," I say as much for her as for me. "Let's go." I hold out my hand, and she takes it. We swim linked together for a few strokes before I break free and paddle on my own. My arms are covered in goose bumps, but by the time I'm halfway out, I've already started to warm up.

"When Cola swims by, hold out your hand and grab on to the part of his dorsal fin closest to his body, okay?" Tara shouts.

I don't see Cola anywhere, but I trust Tara. She bridges, and I remember that dolphins have a super sense of hearing. Suddenly, Cola pops up in front of me. He's enormous, and his smile shows rows of Tic Tac teeth.

"Hey, dude," I whisper.

I feel calm. All those balloon breaths must have carried over.

I let my fingers curl around his fin. Wet suit, windbreaker, rubber-band baby. I hold on tight, and Tara bridges.

Off we go.

We soar through the water and I release a laugh that begins

from somewhere deep inside my heart. It's exactly like I imagined and also nothing like I could have ever expected. I don't know what's going to happen next, but for the time being, I let myself enjoy the moment. Next to Cola, the lagoon feels big, open, wide. Free.

Like home.

Chapter 23

When I arrive in the cafeteria Monday morning, everybody—Socks, Jas, Kisa, Lilly, Ayden, EJ, and Juan Carlos—are gathered around our table staring at something. I wheel toward the tundra side of the table. Lilly tells a story. Something about a crazy thing that happened last weekend. The words *hashtag*, *splash*, and *so cold* filter into my ears. Almost every other word is interrupted with laughter or corrections. I feel my breath catch. Did everyone hang out last weekend without me? Did Lilly have *another* bat mitzvah?

Then I remember. No, of course not. Last weekend we were all together at Dolphina Cove.

I take a low-key balloon breath without even thinking, and listen for a moment to get caught up to speed.

"Dude, your face was so funny! Like—" Ayden pauses and makes an expression of exaggerated, wide-eyed astonishment.

"Whatever. All I'm saying is that my ride was the fastest. They're gonna be calling me 'E to the flash to the J' at Dolphina Cove all year."

"Pshh," Socks says, her cheeks flushing deeper than the most tropical sunset.

Ayden isn't deterred. Like Lilly, he likes to entertain the crowd. Very Cola of him. "I still can't get over that dolphin fur, it felt so—"

"Dolphins don't have fur!" Lilly and I exclaim at the same time.

"OMG, speaking of, I heard they spotted a two-headed dolphin in Turkey," Socks says before popping a handful of blue M&M's into her mouth. That sends us into skeptical hysterics. Where does Socks come up with this stuff?

"Who's *they*?" Jas asks rhetorically.

"No way would I swim with a two-headed dolphin," Kisa admits, speaking to both her cell phone and the group.

"I almost didn't swim with a normal dolphin!" Ayden practically shouts. "Those dudes are mad big and have like four hundred teeth! How do you know they wouldn't eat me right up?"

Jas and I instantly make eye contact and share a quick smile before I interject, "Um, hate to break it to you, but dolphins don't use their teeth for chewing. They swallow their fish whole."

The rest of the squad looks my way.

"That's what I've been telling them!" Jas says, giving me a high five. "Dolphins don't eat people 'cause they don't even chew! Nothing to be scared of! Y'all, KT is like the world expert on dolphins." I blush, because Jas says it in a way that's definitely, no-doubt-about-it, a compliment. "Seriously, you should write a book about them!"

"*The Wild Dolphins of Iowa City*!" Juan Carlos suggests wistfully, before cracking up. I laugh along with him.

"That's mad ridiculous," Kisa says without looking up. I'm learning that she actually seems to pay more attention when her nose is buried in her phone. Kinda like doodling helps me focus or calms me down if I've got something on my mind, maybe.

And yes, Juan Carlos's title is totally ridiculous, but it does give me an idea. A potentially amazing idea for the piece I do still have to write, that's in fact due at the end of the week. Which gives me another maybe not-so-ridiculous idea . . .

"Listen up, everyone," I announce. "I need your phone numbers. My birthday is coming up, and I'm having a thing. Not sure what it is yet, but it's unlikely any marine mammals or their teeth or *fur* will be involved. You're all invited."

"Sweet," Lilly says, snatching my phone first. "Birthday celebration season!" She passes my battered smartphone around the table, and as the recap about our time at Dolphina Cove resumes, my friends enter their digits, one Florida area code at a time. The bell rings, indicating the end of lunch. Ayden scampers after Jas, and Socks, Lilly, and Kisa moan about the burden of seventh-grade science as they sling their backpacks over their shoulders.

EJ fishes a crumpled worksheet out of his backpack and jets out the door in a panic.

Before I see it coming, Juan Carlos captures my phone from where EJ left it on the table.

"Hold up," Juan Carlos says. I watch a piece of his hair fall across his forehead as he plugs his number into my contacts. "I texted myself so I have yours, too."

He smiles, and then shoots me a goofy look. I'm about to respond with my signature KT Wynn look, but my emerging grin is too big to conceal.

I drop my phone in my lap and speed off to fifth-period civics. Once I'm parked in my cutout desk and snuggled inside my emergency hoodie, I think to check my last outgoing text. The text Juan Carlos sent to himself from my phone. Something tells me it might be interesting.

I'm not wrong.

KT Wynn: salsa with a side of punk rock.

Because Mr. Lewis has his back turned, and also because I can't resist, I type back Xylophone appetizer.

Then, at record speed, I pop out one more message, this one to my favorite dolphin trainer: Tara! Hi! Favor . . . too much to explain . . . call you after school? Give Cola a belly rub for me!

Chapter 24

My thirteenth birthday is on a Saturday. I wake up before my alarm. That's like a rule of birthdays. For me, at least. I don't want to waste my special day sleeping. I do one final proofread of my article and email it to Miles. Right on time. I was up until two a.m. poring over my interview notes and writing, typing quicker than Socks talks. Or, almost as quick.

The storm that raged the night before brought nothing but the sunniest skies for the first day of thirteen. Sunshine pours in through my windows, spotlighting a collage of photos and newspaper cutouts that Lucy helped me hang on the wall.

A barrage of texts from Cady and Kaytee arrive before I've had breakfast. They want to know what I'm doing to celebrate. I stick with the same line I've said since I came up with my idea and text it back in all caps:

SURPRISE!!

Not all surprises are bad.

Be ready, 3 p.m. sharp. Keep your phones charged.

Lucy used her graphic design skills (apparently, they go hand in hand with video game skills, who knew?) to make a digital flyer with little GIFs that move. I texted the invitation to my Fernbank Middle squad individually. Mom, Dad, Lucy, and I arrive at the beach an hour early to stake out a spot halfway between the parking lot and the ocean. Sprinkle, bless her heart, can't handle the sand, so Dad gives me a piggyback ride to the king-sized blanket Mom and Lucy laid down. The sky is blue, the clouds are cotton balls, the water is aqua, and the seagulls are squawking. A classic Florida postcard, but real life.

Everything is set up with a few minutes to spare. The leaves, the hay, the thermos of apple cider. Pumpkins pin down the corners of the sheet. Mom and Dad, like actual champs, made an epic Rice Krispies Treat cake in the design of a tree ablaze with orange and yellow leaves. The sound of the ocean hums in the background. A whisper, not the nervous kind, but calm.

Socks and Jas arrive first.

"OMG, KT!" Socks exclaims when she sees me. "This is genius!"

A banner I made out of a pillowcase held up by old broomsticks waves in the breeze like a flag marking newly discovered territory. My territory, new and old. "Resurrect Fall!" the banner reads.

Everyone else arrives almost on time. Mom and Dad must

take the hint and embark on a long walk down the beach. Dad's arm is over Mom's shoulder, and her hair tangles in the breeze. EJ takes out his Bluetooth speakers and Kisa uses her phone to DJ while we chow down on Tommy's burgers and melty milkshakes. Jas and Ayden hold hands. Lilly basically corners Lucy, making sure to name-drop all the high schoolers she's met through her brother. She has a similar look on her face as Cady and Kaytee when she speaks to my big sister. Socks talks about hermit crabs for seven minutes straight, not stopping to take a single breath, balloon or otherwise. Juan Carlos's camera hangs around his neck, but he doesn't hide behind it. He chugs apple cider, "because this is literally the best thing I've ever tasted," he confesses.

Socks and I are wrapping up a debate about the three most interesting school mascots in history when I feel a tap on my shoulder.

"Happy birthday," Juan Carlos says. He hands me something thin that's been wrapped in newspaper. "I'm not the best at presentation."

I remove the newspaper to find a photograph. No frame, just the print. It's from Socks's birthday party. He must have taken it from the dock right before I got out of the water. The image shows Cola and me in the water, looking into each other's eyes. We're both smiling.

"Florida looks really happy on you, Iowa City," Juan Carlos says. I smile almost as big as in the photo and don't even care that I'm blushing. Nothing I can do about it.

At two fifty-five p.m., I scramble among the folds of the sheet and Tommy's wrappers for my phone. I want to make sure I have a good view of the ocean ready so that Cady and Kaytee get a stellar view of the beach for our video call. I'm about to call them when Lucy sneaks up behind me.

"Cover your eyes," she instructs me. "And no peeking. Sister Secret."

I do as I'm told. A moment later my friends' swirling conversations hush. It must be the sight of the Rice Krispies Treat cake. They've probably never seen one before; it's a very Iowa City birthday tradition.

"I hope it's okay to make a wish already," I joke, gearing up to blow out fourteen candles in one breath (one extra for good luck). I think I hear Socks giggle, and I sense some movement coming toward me—Mom and Dad with the cake, I assume. I'm tempted to peek but . . . Sister Secret. I clamp my eyelids even tighter.

"Okay, open your eyes on three," Lucy says, her voice lively with excitement. "One . . . two . . ."

But before Lucy gets to three, I hear two voices that I know so well, they sound like they're coming from inside my heart.

"SURPRISE!!"

Cady and Kaytee sprint across the sand and tackle me with hugs bigger than any Midwestern sky.

"How? When? Really?" are the only words I can formulate.

"I *told* you I was getting YouTube famous and buying us tickets!" Cady insists.

"Really?" I still can't believe they're here. Cady and Kaytee. In Fernbank, Florida.

"My first sponsor fell through . . ."

"And the second," Kaytee teases.

"But where there's a will, there's a way!" Cady says.

They both cheer, sharing a quick look with my parents.

C2K for life.

I look to Mom and Dad. They shrug their shoulders, like this is all one big happy accident.

"Thank you," I whisper. "Thank you so much."

Their smiles say "Happy birthday" better than words ever could.

"I'm sorry, I'm being so rude. Let me introduce you to my friends!" I say.

Cady and Kaytee are just as outgoing as I remember. Within minutes, they're chummy with the entire Fernbank squad. When Juan Carlos gets up for a cider refill, Cady mouths *He's cute!* in a totally obvious way that everybody else sees, and Kaytee pinches my arm and wiggles her eyebrows. I blush big-time. I'm sure all present company notices, but I realize that I don't mind. Like surprises, there are worse things.

Cady and Kaytee marvel at the sight of the expansive ocean. Kaytee shares photos of early fall foliage along the Iowa River. Socks and Jas both can't believe how grand the University of Iowa buildings look in the background. My heart swells, having experienced the beauty of both landscapes. As festivities start to wind down, Juan Carlos sets the self-timer on his camera. All of us—the best Iowa City and Fernbank have to offer—take photo after photo dog-piling onto the picnic blanket.

Two months ago, I never would have imagined this would be my birthday. It's different than I ever could have predicted, and it's also great. Bring it on, thirteen. After my friends leave, I stay on the beach with Mom, Dad, and Lucy. Cady and Kaytee are a ways down the beach, splashing in the sea and drawing in the sand with their toes. With my family, I nibble on the remains of the cake and gaze at the water. It looks nothing like the Iowa River, but the way the late-afternoon sun dances on the surface feels familiar, a picture that's been part of my consciousness for a long time.

Lucy tugs on my ponytail.

"Look," she whispers. She points out into the ocean to her left. I follow her finger with my eyes. I don't gasp. Instead, I take one long balloon breath, savoring every pixel my eye can take in, and grab her hand in mine.

Two dolphins swim in the distance. Their dorsal fins slice through the water. Maybe they're making bubble rings, maybe they're diving for fish, or maybe they're just playing. They could be the same ones Lucy and I saw that first time we went to the beach. They could be sisters or best friends. Or maybe they've only just met, each traveling from their own world, finding each other for the first time in a new, unexplored ocean.

Just Your Average Tuesday: A Day in the Life of a Dolphin Trainer

KT Wynn, Seventh Grade, Junior Reporter

Dolphina Cove is Florida's oldest dolphin sanctuary, just one zip code over on the Gulf Coast. A total of seven Atlantic bottlenose dolphins are cared for there, swimming, playing, and feeding in a natural, open-water lagoon (think nature preserve, not marine mammal amusement park). This article is composed of interviews with Tara and field notes I made while observing sessions and being behind the scenes. Here is a day in the life of Tara, a veteran dolphin trainer.

5:45 a.m.
Rise and shine! Tara has worked as a dolphin trainer for years now, but she's still not used to these early mornings. Two snoozes later, though, she's up!

6:15 a.m.
Tara has a long, physical day ahead, so breakfast really is the most important meal. Her go-to is a fruit smoothie (secret ingredient: cocoa powder!), eggs, toast, and avocado.

6:45 a.m.
Bag packed with an extra swimsuit and mineral-based sunscreen that won't harm any of the dolphins, Tara steps into her flip-flops and she's off to Dolphina Cove!

6:47 a.m.
Oldies, hip-hop, and a sprinkle of jazz make the perfect pre-Dolphina soundtrack.

7:00 a.m.
Tara arrives at the office. But for Tara, her office is a sprawling dolphin sanctuary equipped with a welcome center, trainers' office, and open-water lagoon that houses not one, not two, but *seven* Atlantic bottlenose dolphins. Though the first visitors won't arrive until 10:30 a.m., Tara has no time to waste. Little-known fact: Dolphin trainers are always on the move prepping and documenting nutrition and care for our dorsal-finned friends.

7:05 a.m.
Did I mention prep? First order of business is organizing fish for that day's meals. Each dolphin will eat about twenty-five pounds a day. I'll let you do the math, but that's a lot of fish! Tara gets to work right away. She has only a couple of hours to wash, weigh, and organize the fish into multiple pails for feeding and treats. Each dolphin receives a specific combination of fishies based on their dietary needs. They even get vitamins, which trainers will carefully stuff into the fish gills.

8:45 a.m.
Tara heads to the trainers' office for a staff meeting, where she meets the two other trainers working that day. Together they discuss feeding schedules, upcoming visits, and any training notes from the day before.

9:30 a.m.

Breakfast! Tara loads her arms with as many buckets of fish as she can carry (Tara has biceps for days) and makes her way down to the lagoon. The dolphins are still able to hunt for their own food because the lagoon barrier allows fish from the wild to swim in, but since they've been at Dolphina, the dolphins have gotten a little lazy (shhh, don't tell them I said that!) and mostly wait to be fed by one of the trainers. Then, after a quick belly rub here, and a high five or two there (another fun fact: Dolphins' pectoral fins—the two on their underside—have individual finger bones inside! Probably from back in dinosaur times when they were land creatures), Tara returns to the trainers' office to prep for the first guest visit of the day.

10:30 a.m.

Tara leads the first visitor session. Two families with little kids and a couple from Spain arrive for a shallow-water encounter, which means they'll get into the water up to their knees. Tara explains important safety info before she walks them down to the lagoon to meet mother-and-daughter pair Luna and Sammy.

Tara and the other trainers use a special whistle called a bridge to communicate with the dolphins. It lets the animals know when they've followed instructions and are in store for a reward (clear Jell-O or more fish!).

12:15 p.m.

Lunchtime, finally! More fish for the dolphins, and anything but fish for Tara. While she eats a peanut butter and jelly sandwich on a picnic bench overlooking the lagoon, she sends a photo of Cola to her mom. Her family lives all the way in New Hampshire.

1:00 p.m.

Time for session number two! A few more guests arrive for another swim. This time, Tara doesn't lead, but plays a backup role instead. She keeps an eye on all the dolphins in the lagoon and lets the other trainers know where the animals are located by shouting "Away!" when one swims out of sight. To give Luna and Sammy a break, Ginger and Cola play with the guests.

2:15 p.m.

Free swim—the best part of the day! Every afternoon Tara and the other trainers get the chance to work one-on-one with an assigned dolphin. Recently, Tara's been bonding with Cola, and today is no exception. Cola has been at Dolphina for only a couple of months, and finally he and Tara are starting to really connect. Trainers use free swim to work on new behaviors (think tricks, but not exactly, because the dolphins aren't actually performing). These sessions are fun for the dolphins because they are very intelligent creatures and need a lot of stimulation to feel engaged and happy.

When Tara gets to the lagoon, Cola and Sammy have already started playing without her! Cola especially likes to make bubble rings in the water, which is when he shoots air out of his blowhole and uses his nose to spin the bubbles into a little ring. It's one of his favorite pastimes, and probably something he did before he came to Dolphina Cove, when he lived in the wild. Tara begins the session by throwing him a full bucket of fish.

Trainers like to begin and end sessions differently every time so the dolphins don't get bored by things becoming too predictable.

3:30 p.m.

Last session of the day. Geared up from the free swim, Cola wows the small afternoon crowd by flipping high in the air and letting a pair of twin girls rub his belly.

5:00 p.m.

Clean-up time. Tara and the other trainers spend the final hours of the day washing the prep area and every piece of equipment until it's sparkling and fresh. Well, maybe not fresh. The scent of fish is pretty constant at Dolphina Cove.

6:00 p.m.

Tara is about to leave when she remembers that she still needs to write notes on the day's activities. She documents details about the play session, including number of guest visits, and how much food each dolphin ate, and she updates the health records with that day's stats.

7:00 p.m.

Home sweet home. Tara is sticky with salt water, has fish scales underneath her nails, and is exhausted, but one thing is clear:

She wouldn't trade this job for anything in the whole world.

Acknowledgments

Orlando Dos Reis, editor supreme, the ride thus far has been zippy, exciting, and more fun by the book. You've been a wonderful captain on this particular dolphin-themed ship. A big thank-you to the entire Scholastic squad: David Levithan, Keirsten Geise, Caroline Flanagan, Courtney Vincento, Jessica White, Priscilla Eakeley, and Erin Slonaker—I am grateful for everyone's work to make this book whole.

To Ali Stroker: for your candid and generous consultation, thank you. I hope KT is a kid you would have liked to read about back in your middle school days.

Thank you Teachers & Writers Collaborative and the Cerimon Fund for supporting my work outside the classroom.

Shout-out to Dolphins Plus and the real-life Tara, the inspiration for Dolphina Cove. My intro to dolphin swimming and care was truly a day of thrills and laughter.

For guidance when researching and writing KT's story,

I found incredible resources online, specifically www.thesqueakywheelchairblog.com, disabilityvisibilityproject.com, wordsiwheelby.com, and "The Accessible Stall" podcast. Finally, thank you to Donna Lowich for all your insight and advice, and to those who take the time and energy to show others your worlds.

And of course, the usual suspects: Megan, Marja, Momma, Dad, and Ham: I'm ever appreciative of your brains and your hearts. Xo.

About the Author

Jessie Paddock is the author of *Gemini Academy, The Crush Necklace,* and *The Secrets Necklace.* She holds an MFA in writing for children from The New School. She has lived in New York City for a while now, although she sometimes misses her hometown of Atlanta. She loves summer, soccer, and ice cream cones with extra sprinkles.